THE PECOS TRAIL

by

Edward Love Johnson

DEDICATION:

This book is dedicated to the memory of
Colonel Stuart Arbuckle
One of the greatest horsemen I have known.

CHAPTER 1

The year was 1868. Texas, like other states whose sympathies had rested with the South, was fighting to shake the curse of strife that had ripped it apart for four long years. It was the War Between the States, and events that had happened during that War, that set the stage for the drama soon to be acted out on the plains of Texas, and across the arid wastelands of the New Mexico Territory.

A mission of vengeance had already consumed two years of Nathan Benson's life, and the climax seemed nowhere near at hand. Yet, all the while he was crossing over thousands of miles of trail in his deadly pursuit, at no time had he wavered from his sworn task--to run to earth and kill Shack Cumby.

Shack Cumby. The man who had gunned down his father.

On this spring morning, he came out of the East with the rising sun, a lone rider on that vast expanse of wild land which fanned south and away from the great bend of the Pecos. He was riding a quarter horse stud, a splendid animal with powerful muscles that bunched and flowed beneath a jet black coat. They swung along in a tireless gait that rapidly ate up the miles of dry and dusty trail.

Benson whistled softly as he swayed with the rhythm of the horse. And, as he had so many times before, he envisioned the final act of his drama, when he would meet Shack Cumby face to face. His russet eyes narrowed. His handsome clean-cut features, hardened beyond his twenty seven years, tightened in a grimace. Unconsciously his hand dropped to check the Colt .44 in a worn leather holster on his hip. He felt the nine notches on the six-gun's grip, but gave little thought to their presence, or to the nine characters who had ridden onto the stage with him at various times and places. They were no more.

Abruptly the stud faltered in his stride. His ears shot forward, even before

Benson heard the firing. At first it was a single shot, then there were many--a fusillade of rifles and the dull roar of short guns all mixed up together. It wasn't an Indian raid this far south of the New Mexico Territory, nor was it a hunting party. It was concentrated, frantic firing and it came from beyond the rise directly ahead.

Instinctively, Nathan Benson drew up, his hand tensing on the reins. He leaned forward to stroke the black neck of the stud, streaked with sweat and dust.

"Better swing south, Partner," he spoke to his stud. "Stay out of trouble for a change."

Talking to the stud was nothing new to Benson. He had talked to him over endless miles of trail that stretched all the way back to Waco. And farther still, to a battlefield just outside of Petersburg, Virginia.

That had been a bad day. A bad day for the Confederacy. A bad day for Benson. As he sat in the saddle, he shifted his weight to ease the pressure on his left hip, where a bit of shrapnel from that battle still lay imbedded.

Yet, that day had been a good day, too. That was the day he had traded his last cache of food to a wounded soldier for the animal he now sat astride. That was the day he had acquired the black stud he now called Partner.

For the past ten days the pair had travelled north, following what had turned out to be a blind lead. It had carried them all the way to the great bend of the Pecos, that steep-banked torrent of a river that swept down out of the New Mexico Territory.

Now, they were quartering back to the south. South and west, cutting to the Butterfield Trail. Circling like hounds to pick up the lost scent of a fox.

Benson pulled up. The man who rode that black stud was not adept at running from trouble. A gun battle in this wild and uninhabited land was far too great a temptation for his curious mind. He turned back to the north, heading to the gunfire.

One of the animal's pointed ears thrust out toward the firing. The other lay back along his close-trimmed neck, reading the actions of his rider. The animal heard the heavy breath of decision. His muscles tensed. As he felt the man's weight shift forward, he bunched his quarters and lunged out. His sensitive neck told him that the reins had been knotted and dropped over the saddle horn, giving him freedom of pace. He thundered away, eager for this chance to unlimber his trail hardened muscles. The man's knees would cue him on direction.

Benson rode with his mount, flowing across the sage-dotted earth as though he were a part of the animal itself. He pulled his hat down against the wind and leaned forward. Loosening the lashings on his 1851 Henry repeating carbine, he withdrew the rifle from the saddle boot. He levered a shell into the chamber, then let it ride across the pommel of the saddle.

"Steady boy," Benson spoke into the wind. "Steady Partner."

The stud slowed his pace as he swept up a small arroyo to the crest of the rise. He felt the stirrups shoved forward. Rocking back on his heels, his steel shod hooves cut deep into the hard earth.

From the height of the rise, Benson surveyed the scene of battle. It was an old story, as old as the West -- no doubt much older. A handful of drovers, fighting for their herd and their lives, were badly outgunned by a rustler gang. The outlaws circled just out of pistol range, pouring rifle fire on the trail riders. Back up the trail from this small band, three trail riders lay sprawled on the ground where they fell, the fight already ended for them. Another, hit, but still in the action, propped himself on an elbow, firing his rifle at the rustlers. The rest of the drovers, save one, threw frantic but highly ineffective rounds from handguns.

A second rifle, the only other visible to Benson, was in the hands of a black haired woman on a red roan horse. Benson watched her empty the rifle, quickly and expertly reload, and commence firing again. She rode the flank of the frightened herd, pounding full speed to the north -- riding full onto the scene of battle.

Other riders, one a big man with a flaming red beard, cut out of the dust of the drag to join the fight. Benson could see that the big man also held a rifle. He rocked his big blood bay back in a sliding stop. Taking deliberate aim, his first shot emptied a rustler saddle. Then, he quickly maneuvered the bay, avoiding the hail of lead directed toward him.

Benson had come in behind the gang. How many there were he did not know, but when the guns were going, you didn't stop to count heads. He had learned that from General Fritz Lee at Chancellorsville, and again at Petersburg.

Benson held his rifle ready. He held his fire until the stud came to a full stop, then waited a moment longer. The rustlers milled about, making moving targets of themselves. Three swung out on the grade below him. Benson fixed his sight on the first of them. When they cut in close, he fired. His aim was careful, and the spacing of his shots deliberate. Four times he squeezed the trigger. Four shots. Three riderless horses quartered back around the slope.

Another rustler, seeing the empty saddles, turned toward Benson's position. He saw his three comrades, sprawled on the hillside. Then he saw the black stud and the rider with a smoking rifle. He threw off a quick shot at Benson, at the same time bellowing loudly to his comrades. Spinning about, the rustler sent his mount lunging toward a greasewood thicket a quarter mile away. The others followed, riding low over their ponies like Comanche warriors. One fired a hasty but wild shot over his shoulder. The others concentrated only on their frantic race for cover.

With the outlaws out of range, the trail riders held up their fire.

Benson lifted his rifle. He singled out the one rustler who seemed to be the leader. It was a long shot for a moving target. He drew a careful bead, giving leeway for windage, estimating elevation.

Benson fired.

The sound of that single shot was flat after the roar of battle. The rustler slumped forward, but clung to the saddle horn. He was still up when his horse disappeared into the thicket.

Partner, well accustomed to battle and the firing of guns, had not moved. Benson lowered his Henry. Its octagonal barrel was warm to his ungloved hand. He took five shells from his vest pocket and fed them carefully into the magazine. Dropping the rifle back into the boot, he lashed it back into place.

For a long moment he sat there, breathing in the quiet that followed the riotous burst of gunfire. It was a quiet broken only by the muffled rumble of fleeing cattle, as the dust of the drag climbed away to the north.

Down below, the chuck wagon turned. The driver on the high seat cracked a bull whip over the rumps of the team to send them lunging back toward the outlying injured rider. As more of the scattered drovers trickled in, the woman with the jet black hair and the man with the red beard attended to the wounded man. And he was, in turn, barking orders to those about him.

Benson took his makings from his shirt pocket, rolled a smoke, and touched a match to it. He had done all he could do to help. The battle was over, the rustlers long gone. All that remained to be done was to bury the dead and gather the longhorns back into a trail herd. There seemed to be sufficient help to do that.

He could turn south and west again. With luck he would make the Butterfield Trail in ten to twelve days. From there he could continue his search for Shack Cumby -- a search that had sharpened his gun hand and left his name on every trail from New Orleans to Laredo, across the border and back again. Now it was taking him toward the New Mexico Territory, maybe even to California.

Over the years, he had taken a job here, another there, enough to keep some change jingling in his jeans. Occasionally, there had been a little extra to stow in the pocket of his money belt. But he had always turned again to the trail. Somewhere out there, he would find another lead. He always had. And finally, at the end of one of those little side roads, he would cross the path of his father's killer. He had to. The whole world wasn't big enough to hide the man -- not when the purpose of his search was as strong as that which burned in the breast of Nathan Benson.

He lifted the reins to turn the stud, then lingered a moment. There was something about that woman, the one with hair the color of a raven's wing. It held him -- a moment too long.

He sent his mount loping down toward the wagon.

CHAPTER 2

Jan Raphael was a big man, broad shouldered, raw boned. He reminded Nathan Benson of his father, Saul Benson, as he watched the dark haired woman and the red bearded man attend to his wounds. The man's thick neck bulged. His chest heaved. At intervals, he would shove himself up on his elbows, barking orders to his cowhands.

"Buell, get shovels from the wagon and bury the dead. Take a couple men to help you." Raphael grimaced with pain as he eased back.

A wiry little man with a thin face and steely blue eyes, eyes filled with danger, eyed Benson from his saddle.

With a single sweeping glance, Benson sized up the man, just as he did any likely gunman. He noted the handle of the heavy six-gun thrusting up out of the little man's holster, placed so it would strike the heel of the man's thumb when his arm was fully extended. The holster was tied to his leg with a leather thong. The man's long curved fingers never strayed far from the holster. This man Buell would be a hard man to reckon with in a gun fight. But he would be a good man to have on your side when the going was rough. Benson was sure of that.

Buell found the shovels and turned about.

"Just our men?" he asked.

"Hell yes, just our men!" Raphael spat out. "Leave those rustlers on the hill for the coyotes."

Raphael's hard brown eyes flashed up. He swept the circle, making a hasty survey of riders.

"Hagerman, anyone with the herd?"

"No sir."

The slender man straightened in the saddle.

"Gunfire sounded so hot here, we all turned back. Figured we were needed more here."

The slender man's soft voice and mild manners branded him as out of place on a drive such as this. Benson noted that there was no gun on his hip.

"Well," Raphael said. "Get some men and see if you can turn them before they run all the way to the Territory."

Hagerman turned his horse, speaking softly to the men behind him. The five riders reined up. They were gaunt men with deeply lined faces. Four turned to follow Hagerman, as he loped north after the longhorns. The fifth horseman hesitated for a brief instant, his piercing, almost black eyes on Benson. Then he whirled and galloped away.

Banson watched that fifth rider. The bearded, unshaven face struck no memory chord. It was only those piercing black eyes. The man seemed to recognize him. Somewhere, those eyes had seen him before. Benson was certain of that. He just couldn't place where, or when it could have been. The man might be a gunman he had left for dead along some trail. Maybe the brother of one.

Unconsciously his right hand dropped down to check the gun on his hip. He was still seeing those eyes as he turned back to the wounded man.

"Damn you, O'Quinn," Raphael snorted. "Don't cut my boot."

Raphael's broad face flared as the red bearded man slipped a sheath knife down inside Raphael's boot and split it all the way to the instep.

"That was a new boot!"

"Afraid you won't be needing it for a while, Boss," O'Quinn said.

"At least, I won't die with both of my boots on," the big man sighed.

O'Quinn unbuckled the big man's chaps. "No sir, you won't now.

"Let's get rid of this bloody old trouser leg." O'Quinn continued to talk as he worked. "Can't have the boss looking like he's been in a bar room brawl."

He threw the boot aside and straightened the trousers gently with the help of the woman. He split the trouser leg up past the bullet wound and cut it off.

Raphael winced as he saw the exposed wound.

"Stupid idiot," he said. "That was a good pair of britches."

Raphael looked up at Benson, who had twisted in the saddle and now sat with his left leg locked around the saddle horn.

"Didn't get your name, young man," he said. "I'm Jan Raphael. We're much obliged for your assistance."

His face had grown ashen and his effort to turn his attention from the wound was obvious.

Benson liked the man at once. His face was hard but honest. His eyes were open and clear, with nothing to hide. And there was something commanding about his voice when he spoke.

"Didn't give it," Benson said with a trace of a smile. "But it's free for the asking. Benson. Nathan Benson, from no place in particular."

Jan Raphael's eyes brightened. O'Quinn stood up and crossed to the stud.

"Didn't think I'd ever be so happy to see Nathan Benson."

He thrust out his hand.

"Or should I say, Kandee?" he added. "I'm Nardi O'Quinn."

O'Quinn's red bearded face spread in a broad grin.

"I'd guessed as much." Benson shook O'Quinn's offered hand. "I've heard of you. They told me in Stockton you were on a drive up this way."

"Glad you came by," O'Quinn said. His grin faded. "Those scalawags were giving us a rough way to go. They came close to taking the whole herd and our scalps with it."

The woman looked up at Benson briefly. Her hair fell in dark coils about her face. She brushed it back with a flip of her hand.

"Glad you decided to join in on our side instead of theirs," she said. "You're mighty handy with a long gun."

O'Quinn turned to the woman. "This lady here is Mr. Raphael's daughter, Lore."

She turned her attention at once back to the wounded man, while Benson was still floundering for words.

"And that old goat yonder is Skip Bonner," O'Quinn continued.

The driver came around the wagon. Bonner's ancient face looked like a piece of rawhide that had been exposed too long to the Texas sun. Cook, teamster and trail doctor, he had dragged out a spare wagon bow and cut it into splint lengths. Benson noted the bony, long fingered hands that carried the splints.

He carried a box of medical supplies tucked under his arm. Bonner moved as though his entire being was completely captivated by the task at hand. He showed no interest in small talk, no interest in Nathan Benson, Kandee or whoever else he might be. He didn't bother to look up, but went right to work on Jan Raphael's wounded leg.

Skip Bonner already had a fire going under a pan of water. He bathed the wound and dressed it, his rough hands moving deftly. His face contorted with each action. He handled the big man as gently as a father might handle a child. He muttered to himself as he worked, straightening the leg, aligning the shattered bone, and preparing the leg for the splints.

Skip slipped a flask from his inside coat pocket and passed it to Jan Raphael.

"Take a good snort," he said. "It'll help with the pain when we start tying in the splints."

O'Quinn turned back to help Lore and Skip with the splinting. Benson dropped the reins to ground tie the stud and stepped down from the saddle to lend a hand. They wrapped the pieces of wood with cloth and bound them in to firm up the leg, leaving an opening above the wound so it could be dressed without removing the splints.

"Where are you driving to?" Benson asked, as they tied in the ends of the splints.

"Fort Sumner," Raphael replied.

"Up through the Territory?"

"Yes. Up the Pecos." He winced as they drew the cloth strips down close about the knee. "We're keeping to the west bank as far as possible. Want to keep out of Comanche land. Hear they're a little on the rough side."

"Is there a market there?" Benson raised his eyes to meet the steady gaze of the rancher.

"The Army's buying cattle on the hoof for the Reservation Indians," Raphael said.

"I heard they rounded up some of the Apache tribes," said Benson.

"Yep," said Raphael. "And now they've got to feed them."

"How many head did they order?"

"No order," Raphael said. "But we think they'll take them all."

"You think they'll take them all!" Benson whistled softly through his teeth. "You mean you're driving up by the Apaches and through Comanche land, on a trail that no one has made yet, and you think they will take them?"

"No market there, we'll keep driving." There was determination in the man's voice.

"You've got a bad stretch ahead." Benson stood up and looked to the north where the cattle had long since vanished. "You're short on firepower. You'll need more rifles for sure when you're spotted by a war party."

"It's not just rifles I need," Raphael said. "Mister, I've got three dead drovers lying in the dust out there, and me knocked out of the drive with this busted leg. I'm short of manpower."

"This may not be the last outlaw gang you'll encounter, either," Benson said. "Seems that cattle rustling has become big business. Not just in Texas, either. With the trail you're leaving, every rustler between here and Colorado will be after your herd."

"No matter, we'll make it," Raphael said. "We've got to. We West Texas ranchers need a shorter route to market than the Chisholm Trail. I intend to see we get it!"

"As for rifles, there's seven outlaws up on the slope that won't be needing theirs anymore," Benson said. "Why don't you send someone up to get them and their amunition?"

Raphael looked around. His eyes paused on Tram Donnel, an ex-gambler and gunman from the border country, a cowman now. Already Donnel had stepped into the saddle.

"I'll go," he said, his steel gray eyes sweeping the greasewood thicket where the rustlers had sought cover.

"Weaver!" Raphael called out.

A lean, range-hardened black man came forward. Raphael held out his rifle.

"Take my rifle and cover Donnel."

Kirk Weaver, the only black man on the drive and one of the only two regular J-Bar-L hands on the trail, took up the rifle, eyeing it fondly.

"Yessir," Weaver said. "Those guns might be a lot of help later."

He worked the lever to make sure there was a live round in the chamber, then swung into the saddle and followed Donnel.

When the splinting was finished, O'Quinn called in Gregg Buell to help lift Raphael into the wagon. They removed the tail gate and, working gently, lifted Raphael into the wagon, placing him on a straw tick bed.

"We could use another hand." Raphael looked out through the opened flaps of the covered wagon as Benson gathered Partner's reins.

"Sorry." Benson checked the cinch and turned to the wounded man. "I'm on a job now. Otherwise I'd be happy to talk to you."

"I'd pay a hundred flat for the balance of the trip," Raphael said. "Plenty of grub and the open sky to sleep under."

"I'm travelling southwest," Benson said, looking out across the plains. "You're going north. Take me too far off course."

O'Quinn and Buell mounted and rode north on the broad trail left by the cattle. Donnel and Weaver came in with the rustler rifles.

"Keep one for yourself," Raphael said to Donnel as the cowman slid the rifles into the wagon.

"Didn't have money for a Christmas present for you last season," Raphael addressed Weaver. "I want you to have my rifle. Bonner, get him a box of shells out of the chest."

The hard lines about Weaver's mouth softened. He turned the gun in his hands, eyeing it fondly.

"I've wanted a rifle of my own for a long time," he said, smiling at Raphael. "Can't think of a better time to get one than right now."

Weaver and Donnel mounted and rode off to help with the herd. Still, Benson lingered.

"One of the men we're burying out there is Pete Runion. He was my ramrod," Raphael said gravely. "And with me laid up this way, I'm in a sorry fix."

"You've got some good men here." Benson gestured out toward the men riding north. "You couldn't do any better for a new ramrod than O'Quinn, unless I'm badly fooled."

"I agree with that," Raphael said. "I tried to get him to ramrod before I signed on Pete Runion. But he won't have it. "

Benson gathered his reins and swung up into the saddle.

"Maybe he'd change his mind," Benson said. "Now that the situation has changed."

"He lost a herd once," said Raphael. "He made it clear when he signed on, he wanted no part of a boss job. I didn't ask him anymore about it, and he didn't tell me."

"Donnel looks like a good man."

"He's a good man for the job he's doing. But the men don't respect him proper. We're not paying big wages -- not enough to hold the men if they don't respect the man who gives the orders."

"Sorry I can't help," Benson lifted the reins.

"I'll make that two hundred if you'll ramrod," Raphael said. His hard brown eyes held to the man on the stud. "And double that if the steers bring more than eighteen dollars a head at Sumner."

Lore Raphael had been stooped over the end of the wagon, helping Bonner stop the bleeding which had been aggravated by moving the big man. She turned now to face Benson.

She was taller than he had guessed when he first saw her from the crest of the slope. When he looked into her deep brown eyes, he thought of chestnuts falling from satined burs. A thick mass of raven hair fell over her shoulders, drifting in loose strands around her face.

"We need you, Mr. Benson," she said. "And we need your gun. If Dad's offer isn't fair, name your price."

Their eyes met. Benson smiled as he thought of the song he had been singing, all along the maze of trails across Texas, to New Orleans, and down into Mexico and back.

"There are eyes so brown when the sun goes down; when I find them I'll roam no more."

Surely the eyes of this woman before him were the brown eyes of the song. They were unabashed, as direct and honest as her words.

Then, as suddenly as it had appeared, the smile left Benson's face. His brow knotted and little wrinkles formed over the bridge of his nose. For an instant, his eyes left those of Lore Raphael and trailed out past the horizon -- out to the southwest.

Only an instant, then his eyes came back to Lore. A woman who was strikingly beautiful, even in the working clothes of a range hand. He felt a strange dignity and strength in her presence and it overwhelmed him.

"The offer seems fair enough," he said.

His eyes still clung to the slender, dark haired woman.

"When do I sign on?"

Even in his pain, Jan Raphael smiled broadly.

"Your word is good enough for me, Benson," he said. "Consider yourself signed on!"

"How well do you know your men?" Benson directed the question at Raphael, yet his eyes still clung to Lore.

"As well as could be expected. Weaver and Hagerman are regular J-Bar-L hands." The big man frowned. "The rest are a hard lot, Benson. Washed out gamblers, ranchers, and miners, mostly.

"Can they be counted on?"

"They'll stick by you when the going gets rough, if that's what you mean."

"I'm not so sure about Scoop Haley," Lore said.

"Scoop Haley?" Benson asked. "How much do you know about him?"

"Haley?" Raphael said. "Not much. He came on with O'Quinn."

"O'Quinn vouched for him?" Benson asked.

"Not rightly, as I recall," said Raphael. "Seems they had trailed together before, was all. You've got to remember, we were hard up for drovers."

"He strikes me as a peculiar hombre," said Benson.

"He's got a temper, all right," said Raphael.

"Anything else?" Benson asked.

"I heard one of the hands say he did some hard time before the war," said Raphael. "Gunned a man down. Said it was self defense, but the jury didn't see it that way."

Benson sat in the saddle, silent.

"Say, what's your interest in him, anyway?" Raphael asked.

"Just curious about who I'll be working with," said Benson.

"Well, whatever else he is, he's a top hand with horses," said Raphael. "He handles the remuda. Like I said, I needed men. I couldn't be picky."

"Who was that last man who rode out with Hagerman?"

"Didn't notice," Raphael frowned. "What did he look like?"

"Thin face, with a beard." Benson said. "He had dark eyes. Black, almost."

"That's Buttons," Lore spoke up. "I gave him that name because his eyes reminded me of shoe buttons."

"What's his real name?" Benson asked.

"Hal Hankins," Lore replied. "He says he got shot up pretty bad in the war."

"That can turn a man bitter," said Benson. "Is he a good hand?"

"Since the war, he's been a gun slinging saddle tramp, mostly," said Lore. "Donnel came across him at a bar in Stockton. I don't know where he learned his trade, but it turns out he's a top hand."

Benson ran the name Hal Hankins through his mind, but came up with a blank.

"You'll need every man you have," Benson said. "Even Scoop Haley and Buttons."

"You mean, you'll need them," Raphael corrected him. "I'll be riding this wagon for the rest of the trip. As of right now, I'm turning the job of shoving this herd through to Fort Sumner over to you."

Raphael turned his attention to Lore.

"Now, girl," he said. "Let's get this wagon rolling!"

"You're not going anywhere until I finish dressing this wound!" Lore said.

"First," Benson said, "I'll need to get a handle on this job."

"You'll get lots of support from O'Quinn. You said it yourself, you can't beat him."

"I'll be depending on him to show me the ropes," Benson said.

"He'll do anything he can to get you squared away," said Raphael. "Anything but ramrod, that is."

"One more thing," said Benson. "This is new country to me. You got anybody that knows their way around these parts?"

"When we catch up with the herd, have O'Quinn introduce you to old LaRoche. He's our scout. Only ones that know this country any better are Mescalero or Comanche."

Lore finished with the wound and stood up. She turned to face Benson.

"Do you think that gang will give us any more trouble?" she asked.

There was concern in her voice, but no fear.

Benson looked for a long time into the eyes of this strange woman. A woman he had watched work tenderly over Jan Raphael. Yet, only minutes earlier he had seen her ride into battle with her gun blazing.

"Probably not," he said, as he looked across the draw to where the rustlers had taken cover. "I figure they went through that thicket and kept going."

"If that's the case," she said. "They could be miles away by now."

"They played their hand, and they lost," Benson said.

"I think they haven't quite figured you out," Lore smiled.

"What makes you say that?" Benson asked.

"I imagine they're still wondering how you got behind them without being seen."

"Well, we'll keep alert anyway," Benson said. "Just in case they get bold again."

Lore turned and walked to the front of the wagon. Benson's eyes followed her every movement. He realized suddenly, that even the sight of her created a strange thrill inside him. It was not the old desire to possess, to use. It was different, new, and a little frightening to a gunman with a job to do.

Lore returned shortly with a Bible bound in worn white leather.

"I'll read over the graves," she said. "Will you join me?"

CHAPTER 3

They gathered the longhorns back into a trail herd, and bedded them down on the plains two full days south of the Territory. O'Quinn and Benson made a head count. They had lost more than a hundred head in the raid.

Donnel and Wink Wellman, a rancher before the war, a hand to mouth cowman now, had drawn first nighthawk shift. As they rode the rim of the herd, night came down out of the hills, closing in about them.

A black stud drifted into the encampment out of the shadows. Benson dropped rein near the wagon. He walked into the circle of light around the camp fire. Weary riders sat on the ground or hunched on their heels with plates of steaming beef and beans.

Benson paused where O'Quinn sat.

"I want the guard doubled tonight," said Benson.

"It'll mean every man riding a shift," said O'Quinn. "I'll take mine too. Put me in where you need me."

Kirk Weaver looked up, his sheepskin jacket open to the fire.

"You expect more trouble from that gang?" Weaver asked.

"No," Benson said. "But if they come looking for it, we'll be ready for them."

"If they've got a hankering to get brave again," said Weaver. "I'm itching to try out my new long gun."

O'Quinn stood up. Firelight danced on his red beard. The heavy brows grew a frown.

"I already mentioned doubling the guard," he said. "But it didn't go over so big."

Benson had started toward the cook pots. He paused, a plate and cup in his hands. He turned slowly, his russet eyes growing a shade darker as they swept the circle.

"Didn't go over big with who?" he asked.

Scoop Haley stood up. His beady eyes burned out of deep sockets.

"Me for one," he said. "I signed on to wrangle the horses. That's what I aim to do, until Mr. Raphael tells me different."

"I'm ramrod of this drive now," Benson's voice was even, deliberate, but it carried an edge. "And I'm telling you different. You'll take the shift O'Quinn signs you to."

The wrangler's hand dropped to the butt of his gun. It held there, the fingers not closing yet. Benson made no move. Already he had shifted the plate and cup to his left hand. His right hung free, just above the butt of his Army Colt .44.

Donnel, caught in line between the two men, rose quickly and stepped back. Dexter Hagerman, his face ashen white, spilled his coffee as he stumbled away from Haley.

Benson's eyes danced like live coals. They held, unwavering, dead on the wrangler. The flat planes of his face were a featureless mask.

"You started for your gun," he said, his tone as chill as the breeze that had come in with the night. "Are you going to take your shift, or go for it?"

For a moment Haley hesitated. The men lowered their plates, their hunger forgotten. The wrangler's expression barely changed. He turned ever so slowly. His hand moved away from the butt of his gun. He strode to his horse, casting one fierce glance back at Benson before he mounted. He whipped his reins viciously on his mount's neck, and rode out toward the herd.

Benson gazed around the circle. The silence was deafening.

"Anyone else?" he asked.

Benson turned back to the fire. He ladled the beans and beef onto his plate and filled his cup with the witches brew that Bonner called coffee. He walked back across the circle to squat beside O'Quinn.

"Most of the men are as concerned as you and me," O'Quinn said.

He paused a moment, then spoke again.

"I'm curious," O'Quinn said.

"Spit it out," said Benson.

"Why didn't you go ahead and part his hair with that .44 when he started for his gun?"

"We need him," Benson said. "Need every man we have."

"Well, you'd best keep a watch on him," O'Quinn said. "He carries a grudge. And he's fast. Faster'n all hell."

. . .

Later, as day came to the western plains of Texas, Benson watched the longhorns feed out and trail north. He guided Partner up the flank of the herd to the point where O'Quinn rode.

"Hold them in close to the Pecos," he said. "LaRoche tells me the grass is better there."

"What about those mountain streams feeding the river up ahead?" O'Quinn asked.

"When we get to them, we'll swing back to the plateaus. They'll make a better crossing for the wagon."

"Makes sense to me," O'Quinn said, as he turned his mount northeast and signaled the flank guards.

Benson dropped back as the longhorns swung by, scattering across the plain, feeding as they moved. There was an occasional bellow of protest, followed by a shrill "Yiii! Yiii!" as the cowboys urged along any reluctant strays. The sun burned a scorching path across the sky. By the time they made camp in a protected draw, it had already dropped behind the high ground to the west.

When the old scout, LaRoche, came in from his daily foray, Benson talked with him briefly. Then, he called the riders together.

"I heard rumors back in Stockton about border outlaws," he said. "LaRoche tells me we'll cross the border tomorrow. We'll keep the guard doubled until we are two full days into the Territory."

Once again, day crawled out of the east and the herd swung north. They crossed the border without incident. A week passed without any further event, then another. The trail riders cursed the heat, the sweat, and the dust that caked their bodies.

"Sand even gets into the grub," Dexter Hagerman complained.

They reached the Rio Felix and drove on west -- crossed that river in the late evening and turned north once again. North to the Rio Hondo. They were a full day west of the Pecos now.

Tempers grew edgy with the monotony, as short as the water supply in this arid land they crossed.

Then, at the end of the first day out from Rio Hondo, as night came down out of the mountains and raced across the mesas, LaRoche crept in, as silent as the dusk. He stepped down from his blue roan that seemed so near a part of the night.

"Indians," he said bluntly.

As the trail riders crowded around, the old scout told of a pair of Mescalero Apache scouts who had shadowed the movement of the herd briefly that afternoon.

"Maybe a war party," he said.

"Could they just be scouting for a hunting party?" Lore asked the old scout.

"Whichever, it don't matter none," LaRoche said. "Their interest is now in beef."

"You think they'll attack tonight?" Lore asked.

"Not tonight," he said. "I figure early morning."

"What do we do? Just wait for them?"

The old scout was as unemotional as though he was reporting on a herd of buffalo.

"They don't know I seen them," he said. "I followed them to their camp.

Know where they'll spend the night. I'll look in on them and let you know something by morning."

He turned to Benson.

"Something strange," he said. "They seemed to be checking another trail at the same time they were watching the herd. I didn't quite get it."

LaRoche had finished his say. He slipped the bridle so the mare could graze while he ate. After he had finished his dinner, he sat for more than an hour, gazing into the cook fire, watching the embers die one by one. When at last he stood up, he seemed rested.

LaRoche took the big Sharps rifle from his saddle boot and slid it into the wagon.

"Too heavy for night work," he told Raphael. Then he unbuckled the sheath knife on his belt, lifted himself into the saddle, and rode into the night.

Benton turned back to finish bedding down his stud. He had loosened the cinch earlier. Now he removed the saddle and placed it where he intended to bed down. He was ready to slip the bridle when he saw Buttons coming toward him, those nearly black eyes shifting -- first to him, then to the stud.

Benson swung around. He had seen the man studying him on several occasions. There seemed to be no menace in his approach, yet Lore had referred to him as a gunslinger.

"Fine animal you have there," Buttons said as he drew close. "Couldn't help admiring him."

His eyes were on the stud now. He ran a hand down the stud's back, grasped the tail and walked around his rear. He touched the inside of the right hock gently.

"He's got a scar there," said Buttons.

Then, he straightened, facing Benson.

"Now what do you suppose caused that?"

Benson's brow knotted.

"Shrapnel," Benson said slowly.

Benson watched the man's expression soften, a trace of a smile cross his face.

"Captain Kandee," Buttons said. "Captain Nathan Kandee Benson."

Benson felt a strange tingle up his spine. Captain Kandee. He hadn't heard that since he laid his uniform aside at Appomattox.

"You've got me pegged," he said. "but I can't place you."

Buttons came back around the stud.

"You remember the day you got this animal?"

"Sure. Had my horse shot out from under me at Petersburg. The same day, I traded for Partner here."

"Yep," said Buttons. "I'd wager you both picked up shrapnel that day."

Benson eyed Buttons suspiciously.

"Only one way to know that for sure," Benson said.

"You shot a Yank that day, too," said Buttons. "One who was slicing up a Reb with his bayonet."

"It was a long shot," said Benson. "But I saw him drop."

"He had a sucking chest wound," said Buttons. "Crawled off into the underbrush."

"You were there," Benson said flatly. "You had to be, or you couldn't know any of this."

Benson's right hand inched slowly closer to his holster.

"That Reb," said Buttons. "He was chopped up pretty bad by the time you got there."

"I left him my canteen, and what little food I had," said Benson. "It was the best I could do. We were on the move, and we had to leave our wounded."

"He's the man who gave you this horse," said Buttons, "for saving his life."

"I always figured I was too late to save him," Benson said. "Figured he was cut up so bad he didn't make it."

"Bet you figured that Yank was done for, too, didn't you?"

"How do you come to know all of this?" Benson asked.

His hand was now clearly poised over the butt of his pistol, ready to draw.

Buttons laughed. He held his hands out, palms up.

"You can relax your trigger finger, Captain Kandee," he said.

"Mister," said Benson, "you'd best explain yourself."

"No, you weren't too late to save that Reb," Buttons said. "Matter of fact, you saved him twice. It was nearly a week before a unit of the 14th Virginia retook that spot, and hauled me back behind our lines. If it wasn't for that water canteen, and those vittles you left me, I would have been dead a second time!"

Chapter 4

Off to the north, three hundred miles as the crow flies, twice that distance by a network of trails, a lumbering wagon caravan fought its way through a brief but fierce encounter with a Kiowa war party. Frightened drivers still peered back around canvas covered bows. Some pulled down their lunging teams. Others lowered their whips, and their weary horses dropped back to a trot, then a walk, blowing hard.

Shack Cumby sat on his mount, apart from that long line of wagons crawling like an oversized caterpillar into the west. His great bass voice no longer boomed orders. He lifted a heavy hand to his reins, then lowered it.

"Damn," he exclaimed, to no one in particular.

His voice was low, husky, only half audible. His bull neck bulged as he watched three spiralling columns of black smoke rise back down the trail and sift across the plains.

A lone rider broke out from the hapless band of horsemen who brought up the caravan rear -- mostly cowhands, farmers, and washed-out drifters. Some, he knew, were like himself. Always on the run.

Still, they had stood this first test. He hoped they would do as well on others that were sure to follow.

The lone rider, his leggy pinto bounding across the carpet of green that spring had brought to the plains, was no cowboy or farmer. His tattered buckskin garb branded him a scout.

He rode easily, his gaunt form draped over the saddle horn like a sack of wet feed.

Lance Kimball pulled up where Cumby waited. He looked across the Oklahoma Territory that fanned out and back toward the eastern horizon.

"Lost three schooners," he said.

His voice was calm, no trace of emotion.

Cumby sat silent for a long moment. When he finally spoke, it was with the smoothness of silk and the tension of steel, all wrapped up together.

"I can see," he said. "And I can see they've sacked and burned them."

He lifted his heavy hand again and removed his hat to let the prairie breeze sift through his snow white hair.

"How many men did we lose?"

"Two dead. Tanner and that red-headed gambler. Deskin got bored clean through. We got him in a wagon. He might make it."

"And the women in the wagons that broke down?"

"Two women and a young girl taken captive. Don't think any of them got hit."

"Then we'll go back and get them." There was passion and a measure of fire in his words, booming up out of his massive chest.

"You shoulda stayed in Texas." Kimball studied the back trail. His leathery expression did not change.

"And what do you mean by that?" Cumby half turned in the saddle. Deep lines furrowed his forehead.

"I mean you don't know Plains Indians, is all. You'd best get them wagons as far out of Kiowa land as you can before nightfall. When them heathens get back to camp, they may send out a real war party."

Cumby spat at the ground. The casual manner of this man who had scouted the plains for thirty years irritated him at times.

"This one looked real to me," he said presently.

"They'll have three white-eye captives, six horses and a whole passel of plunder. Likely every brave in the camp will want to count coup on your wagon train."

"I'll take your word for it," Cumby said slowly. "We'll keep them moving."

"I'd best have a look-see out ahead," Kimball said as he pulled his horse around. "Wouldn't be very fittin' to smack into another bit of trouble just yet."

He let out the reins and loped into the prevailing west wind.

Shack Cumby sat for a moment more. He turned his head slowly to the south, out across the plains, plains that lifted and rolled, then dropped away. He had found himself looking south frequently of late.

Kimball was right. He didn't belong in this wild and violent land. He should be in Texas. He wasn't a wagon master. He was a rancher.

But there was Nathan Benson on his trail.

He couldn't go back to Texas. He reined his mount about fiercely and rode off, down the long line of wagons.

"Close up that gap, Billups!" Cumby boomed. "You're making a break in the line!"

Cumby watched the ashen-faced driver whip up his team.

"Braxton, you'd better plug up that bullet hole in your water barrel," he said to the next wagoneer, "before it's drained plumb dry."

He reined in his horse where Tommy Dill had pulled his wagon out of line -- out of the dusty rutted path that was the Sante Fe Trail.

Dill was on one knee beside the off horse, his left hand under the shoulder, just back of the breast strap. When he pulled it out it was covered with blood. A pool of red spread out on the ground between the horse's front feet.

"Took an arrow," Dill said, as he wiped his stained hand on a clump of prairie grass. "Tore one hell of a hole. Cut out through the back of the shoulder. Had to pull it on out. Losin lots of blood and going lame fast."

"Better cut him out," Cumby said. "Turn him go and he may make it. Drive him another mile heated up like that and you'll drain every drop of blood out of him."

"What'll I do?" Dill looked up at the big man. Fear pinched his face and drained blood from his lips. "Old Ben there can't pull the wagon all by himself. Not the way I have it loaded."

"Skin off the harness and be ready when Thompkins comes by. He has spare horses. I'll ask him to drop you one. Then get that wagon moving pronto." Cumby reined up and moved back to the line.

The wagons rolled on, creaking and groaning across the hard earth. Night crawled out of the east behind them and Kimball found a little swale before a stand of tamarack. They would have some protection from the west wind as well as those unpredictable storms that ravaged the plains at this season.

Cumby lifted a hand and the lead wagon swung left. The second followed suit, then the third, and so, back down the line. They circled wide at first, then began to draw tighter and tighter until the inevitable wall of wagons grew a close perimiter about the camp.

As twilight came in, Cumby crossed the inner circle. He moved to a half dozen paces from the lead wagon, where Shank, the cook, had laid his fire with bits of kindling he had gathered along the way.

Cumby poured a cup of steaming coffee from the blackened pot.

"Damnable luck," he muttered.

"What say, Mister Cumby?" Shank asked.

"I thought we had slipped past those Kiowas," he said glumly.

Shank scratched his grey beard, studying Cumby.

"Reckon not," he said presently.

"I can't blame them," said Cumby. "We've taken so much from them already, I hate to shoot them."

"Ain't got no problem with that myself," said Shank, "If'n it's their scalp or mine."

Except for manmade sounds from within camp, the prairie was draped momentarily in that near sacred silence that separates day from night.

Cumby watched Kimball, as silent as the twilight itself, slip between the wagons and drift out into the shadow.

CHAPTER 5

An hour passed. A prairie wolf gave voice to the night, as the scout stepped back into the circle of light from the cook fire. Kimball came to the wagon tongue where Cumby sat with his chin cradled in cupped hands.

Abruptly, the wagonmaster looked up.

"We'll be needing to hold up a day or two and patch up the wagons," he said.

"First, we get out of Kiowa territory," said Kimball.

"How soon you reckon that'll be?"

"Maybe three, four days. Depends on where we find water."

"And on how long these cracked wheels hold out," said Cumby. "What about the Comanche?"

"Fore we get to Sumner, we gotta face 'em," Kimball said.

"There's no way to avoid them?"

"We'd never slip a wagon train this size past them."

"Well," said Cumby, "We fought off the Kiowas. If we have to fight our way through, we will."

"They're stronger than the Kiowas," Kimball said. "More troublesome."

Cumby dropped his hands and stood up. Light from the cook fire played across his face, cast shadows in the deep furrows that time and the Texas sun had wrought in his forehead. His eyes fixed on the old scout.

"You were right this afternoon, Lance," he began. "I don't belong here."

"You got a soft spot for Indians," Kimball said. "Out here, that'll get a man kilt."

"Some day," said Cumby, "I'll tell you why. Right now, I'd a whole lot rather be back in Texas."

"And face up to Nathan Benson?" Kimball asked.

"At least with him, I'd be able to square off and fight."

"Seems to me," Kimball said, "there's plenty of fight right here, if you want it."

"I've got no quarrel with Indians," said Cumby. "These people make me fight them when I don't want to."

They both stared into the embers of the campfire for what seemed to Cumby a long time.

"You think Benson is still on your trail?" Kimball asked at last.

"I know he is," Cumby said, his eyes straying out into the night. "I know he is."

"You really shoot his old man?"

"Yes. I shot him alright."

"Heard Benson's old man was maybe even faster than his boy."

"What I did wasn't anything to be proud of," said Cumby. "Even if Saul Benson was the best rifleman in Texas, or so they tell me."

"It was a fair fight?"

"I thought so at the time" said Cumby. "I knew I was no match for him."

"Why did you go up against him?"

"Fact is, I never had a beef with Saul Benson until Bandy Parker stirred things up between us."

Cumby poked a stick into the dying embers and stirred them around aimlessly. Kimball gave him his lead, and waited for Cumby to resume his story.

"Bandy Parker and his cronies were gobbling up most of the ranches in the valley, but Parker especially had his cap set for Saul Benson's spread."

"I recall the Benson place as being one of the finest spreads in West Texas," Kimball said.

"Not only that," Cumby said. "Saul Benson's place butted right up against Bandy Parker's place."

"Seems to me that between the two," Kimball said, "Benson had the best place by far."

"Parker had always been jealous of Benson's place," said Cumby.

"A better word might be covetous, from what I hear," said Kimball. "I'm plumb sorry, I keep interrupting you. Go on with your story."

"Well, Jake Rawlins, Parker's foreman, started hanging around Saul Benson. It started out harmless enough, Jake buying Saul drinks down at the saloon, and letting on how Saul was such a legend with that Henry .50 caliber of his."

Kimball stood up and walked to the fire. Holding the hot handle with his trail glove, he picked up the coffee pot and poured some into his tin cup.

"Go on," Kimball said, "I'm listening."

He held the pot out to Cumby.

"Care for some?" he asked.

"I've had my fill, thank you," said Cumby. "Anyway, it wasn't anytime until Saul was giving me the evil eye whenever I would pass him on the street. I didn't rightly notice it then. But looking back, it's plain as day."

"You figure Jake Rawlins was pumping Saul Benson full of lies about you?"

"Like I say," Cumby continued, "I didn't catch on then. Now, nothing else explains to me what it all finally came to."

"What was Rawlins telling him?"

"I never knew then, and I don't know now," said Cumby. "All I know, is Saul Benson got to where he looked at me like he was looking at the devil himself. It just festered like that, till one day I came into town to pick up some staples. I had just tied off my horse in front of the General Store, when Saul Benson stepped out into the middle of the street."

"Was he packin' iron?" Kimball asked.

"He was carrying that .50 caliber Henry one handed, slung low, and barrell down to the ground," said Cumby. "I can see it now, like it was just yesterday. And Jake Rawlins was leaning against the wall of the saloon, a toothpick between his teeth, and a big smile on his face."

"What did he say?"

"He called me by name. I held my hands out, palms up, and told him I didn't want any trouble."

"What did he do?"

"He just said, 'You got a gun. I suggest you go for it.' "

Cumby sat, staring into the fire. It was almost out now, and the dying coals cast an eerie red glow onto their faces.

"Go on," Kimball said softly. "End it."

Cumby's voice grew husky. "Isn't much more to tell. Benson brought his rifle up and fired. I was past thinking, I just reacted. I drew and shot, but in the time it took me to get my gun out and fire, Saul Benson got off another round.

"Don't sound like he was much of a rifleman to me," said Kimball.

"But he was," said Cumby. "You know he was. He'd gunned down a dozen men that I know of with that same .50 caliber."

"That's what I always heard tell," Kimball said. "but he missed you two times. Some of these gunslingers cast a big shadow, but it's all hat.'"

"Not Saul Benson," said Cumby. "He was the real article."

"How do you explain it, then?" Kimball asked.

"His shells," Cumby said.

"His shells?" Kimball asked. " What do you mean, his shells?"

"That night, Bandy was celebrating down at the saloon," Cumby said. "He got roaring drunk. He laughed at how he'd got me to kill Saul Benson for him, so Bandy could get his hands on the Benson ranch while Nathan was away. "

"I don't get it," Kimball said. "What's his shells got to do with it?"

"That's the reason Bandy had Jake Rawlins buddying up to Bensons. He was bragging that he had Rawlins switch out Benson's cartridges for a box of duds. They just had enough powder to make a big noise and clear the bullet out of the barrell.

"Sounds like a case of pure self defense to me," Kimball said.

"Sheriff Ray ruled it that way. Fact is, the whole town saw it. Saul Benson ran two shells through that lever action Henry before I got off my first shot."

"Ain't that the dangdest thing I ever heard!"

"Sheriff Ray pried open the rest of Saul Benson's shells. There was just enough powder in them to pop the bullet out of the gun barrel."

"The Sheriff should have arrested Rawlins -- and Bandy Parker."

"Maybe, but he didn't. There was no use. Parker had a lock on the local politics in Waco."

"Sheriff Ray was mad as all Hell over what Parker had done," Cumby said. "But he wasn't about to do anything about it. He kinda hinted that he would look the other way if someone happened to plug Bandy."

"You take the hint?" asked Kimball.

"I did just that."

"That settle it?" Kimball asked.

"Nah, it didn't do no good," Cumby said. "Bandy's boy was as bad as he was, maybe worse. With Saul dead and Nathan Benson off to the war, there wasn't anyone to stop Bandy's boy from taking over the ranch."

His brow knotted and the furrows in his forehead seemed to deepen. "The way it went down, Parker wouldn't fight a square fight, so I had to draw down on him."

"Folks should have got you a medal," Kimball said.

"Well, Bandy's boy was still around," Cumby said. "Even though Sheriff Ray wouldn't miss Bandy too much, he still might feel the need to string me up, if just for the sake of appearances. And then, Benson was bound to come back sooner or later."

"Think I'd have waited til Nathan got home and told him just what really happened."

"No chance." Cumby stared off into the darkness again.

"I reckon not," said Kimball. "He wouldn't have been too keen on your killing his Pa."

"No," said Cumby softly. "Benson's the kind of gunman who shoots first and asks questions later."

"Could be," Kimball said. "Guess that's how he stays alive."

CHAPTER 6

The ears of the black stud thrust up and out, pointing across the valley. The cattle, stirred by the riders, emitted bellows of protest. The man in the saddle straightened. He had learned to read well the actions of his mount. His russet eyes flashed in the grayness of the waning night, but he saw no farther than the near rim of the herd.

The stud took a step forward. Hard muscles rippled beneath his jet black coat. He stepped again nervously and knickered, eager to be off. Nathan Benson lifted his hand to the rein. He rocked his mount back as a red roan came in out of the night to pull up beside him.

"You think they're out there?" Lore Raphael's soft voice was almost lost in the bellow of the cattle and the shouts of the riders as they rousted them out, building the point, hazing in the strays. She looked at the man beside her, a handsome, fine featured man. A hardened gunman. That she knew. Yet she had, of late, tried to convince herself that it was the circumstances of his life that had prompted his profession. She was troubled; heretofore, she had held gunmen in such contempt. Now she found herself trying to excuse this man who the whole west knew and feared.

Benson turned from the herd to meet her probing eyes beneath the loose strands of dark hair. Eyes that clung to him each time they came face to face -- as if to seek out what lay hidden beneath the flat planes of his windburned face.

"They're out there," Benson said. His eyes swept her graceful form, her full rounded breasts, her slender waist. A bone handled .36 caliber Colt rode high on her hip and the lashings had been loosened from her booted carbine.

"They're out there, alright," he said again.

"You think they will come in with the day?" The girl's face was tense. Yet, if fear lurked somewhere down inside her, it was not visible.

"Here's the man who can answer that," he said.

A smoke blue mare paced in out of the shadow. LaRoche stepped down from the saddle as his mount rocked to a stop. He had come by the wagon and the big Sharps rifle was in his saddle boot. He turned his ancient face up to Benson.

"A couple dozen and a few more," he said. "No war paint. A hunting party. Right now they hunt beef."

LaRoche was a blunt man. As blunt as the Crow Indian woman who had borne him, as alert to the trail as the French trapper who had survived the wilds long enough to father him. With the white man's education, the red man's intuition, he was an excellent scout in this wild and untamed land.

"You think they're spoiling for a fight?" Benson turned his eyes back across the valley. His ears strained for the hoot of an owl that wasn't an owl, the broken cry of a coyote that wasn't a coyote.

"No." LaRoche's answer was positive. "They'll avoid it if they can. They shouldn't be off the reservation. All they want is food for their squaws and children. Maybe shoot a rider or two, stampede the cattle and cut out a few head. Drive them to the canyon where their little ones are."

"When?"

"Very soon." The scout turned his eyes to the east where a flare of light was climbing into the sky.

"How soon?" Lore asked.

"They'll come in with the first light of day."

"Where are they now?"

"Broke camp two, maybe three hours ago. I last saw them in an arroyo about a half mile ahead. I think maybe they're planning a big surprise."

"We'll give them a surprise." Benson's voice was even, cold. "And we'll give them their stampede -- before they're ready for it."

"They'll fight."

"So will we." Benson turned to Lore. "How's Jan?" he said. "Think he can handle a few fast miles?"

36

"He rested better last night," she said. "I've got him padded with all the blankets we have. He's ready to run if that is what we have to do."

"That's what we're going to do." Benson's eyes held to Lore -- seeing in her what he had always wanted to see in a woman -- wondering if what he saw was good for a gunman whose fate rested in a hard heart and a fast hand. If Jan Raphael had not picked up a rustler bullet he would not be here. Maybe that would have been better, for the strange feeling of excitement that he experienced each time he looked upon this enchanting range woman was beginning to frighten him.

"Do you think he can take a hard run?" he found himself saying.

"He'll take it." Her voice was quiet but firm. "He said he'd see the herd through to Fort Sumner, come hell or high water. He meant it."

"We should have sent him back to Fort Stockton," Benson said. "The trail up ahead has promise of being an ordeal for even a well man."

"I couldn't have done that to him." Lore looked out across the valley. "This drive is an obsession with him. Seeing it through. Blazing a trail. He wanted to prove to the ranchers in southwest Texas that there was a shorter route to market than the Chisholm Trail."

"And if there's no market at Fort Sumner?"

"LaRoche says there is. If not, we'll drive on up through Raton Pass into Colorado. I hear there's a good market in mining towns up there."

"This may not be the last Indian encounter."

"Then we'll fight them when they come. We don't have a choice."

"You may run out of riders," Benson said. "You lost four in the first fight. We might lose a couple more today. A few to the Comanches farther up. That won't leave many to deal with outlaws on the other end."

"But we have Benson," she said. "Nathan Benson."

He saw little wrinkles form in the corners of her eyes and tiny devils danced in their deep dark depths.

"When we get down to just the two of us," she laughed, "you can ride point, and I'll bring up the drag."

Benson had not seen her laugh before. Even in the tenseness he found himself laughing with her.

LaRoche remounted. He sat slumped in the saddle. Except for the etchings of years, his face was without expression. He did not laugh with Lore and Benson. He gave no evidence of having heard them. But he did hear the rhythmic tattooing of the hooves of the big blood bay as it left the rim of the herd and pounded up to join them.

"We're moving out," Nardi O'Quinn addressed Benson. His hard blue eyes and flame red beard seemed to prematurely reflect the sun, yet hidden beneath the eastern horizon.

"The herd is edgy," he said. "They're ready to run."

"Who have you got on the flanks?"

"Weaver and Donnel. They're out near the point, ready to roll."

"Start them out west until you reach the center of the valley," Benson looked out across the valley. The shades of night were beginning to draw away. "Then turn them north. If we're going to run them, we'd just as well run them toward Sumner."

"How soon?" O'Quinn looked anxiously at the sky.

"I'll give you a quarter hour to get everyone in place," Benson said. "LaRoche thinks we've got trouble ahead, probably an ambush. Maybe we can catch them with the stampede as they come out -- steal their surprise."

He studied the lay of the land that was slowly becoming visible.

Benson looked at Nardi O'Quinn, as if seeing him for the first time. He watched the corners of O'Quinn's blue eyes narrow, a smile spread behind his red beard. If Nardi O'Quinn had ever known fear, it had been long before he filed that seventh notch on the handle of the Colt .44 that hung low on his right hip.

"When you hear two shots," he said, "head them out."

O'Quinn had already wheeled his mount.

"We'll catch them off guard," he said. "We'll run the longhorns smack over them."

He drove spurs into the bay and lunged away.

CHAPTER 7

Lore turned to Benson. "Where do you want the wagon? Skip's getting mighty impatient. He's loaded and ready. Perched on that high seat and raring to go."

"Send him up the right flank," Benson said. "Tell him to keep a safe distance from the cattle. We want the longhorns between him and the Apaches. You'd best ride with the wagon."

"I'll start him off," Lore said. "But then I'll ride with the herd."

"I'd rather you didn't," Benson said. The coldness had left Benson's voice. His eyes lingered on the woman -- a moment too long. He jerked erect. Someday, after he had unravelled the long trail of Shack Cumby -- after he had stuffed enough money in the belt around his middle to buy a ranch. Someday he would look for such a woman as Lore Raphael.

Lore sat her mount in silence, looking at this strange man--seeing the tenseness in his face. Tenseness that he could not hide. She heard the concern in his voice.

"I'll ride with the herd," she said again, softly. "That is where I want to be. It makes me feel like I'm filling Dad's shoes. I know you wouldn't want to stop me."

She whirled her mount and loped away.

"She's a mind of her own," LaRoche said. A trace of a smile crossed his weathered features.

"And it will get her in trouble some day," Benson snapped, the edge coming back in his voice. He loosened the reins, and the stud lunged away.

Riding the rim of the herd, Benson drew his gun, ready to fire. Then his eyes strayed to the crest of a rim off to the left. Two Indian ponies had pulled up. Others were drifting in, two by two, until a long line of warriors stood out on the western horizon.

Benson pulled his mount up, his hand with the six-gun still lingering momentarily over his head. LaRoche, pounding along on the blue roan, paced up beside him. His face, as he looked up at Benson, was without expression.

"What do you make of that?" Benson's voice rose above the noise of the herd.

LaRoche shook his head.

"They don't want a fight," he said slowly. "Otherwise, they would have tried to surprise us."

"What do you think they want?"

"They want beef. We'll soon see how they intend to get it."

Kirk Weaver, bringing up the drag, saw what was happening and spurred his mount up the flank.

"Ride ahead and get help," Benson shouted as Weaver drew near. "Tell them no stampede. Do you hear? NO STAMPEDE!"

Weaver leaned forward on his little cowpony and shouted in its ear. The animal answered with a burst of speed. They watched him pull away. Then, they turned their attention back to the long line of warriors.

Two Indians, the ones who had first appeared on the crest, stepped their mounts forward a few paces and halted. One of the Indians, who carried a long feathered lance and wore an eagle feather in his hair, raised his right hand to the sky.

"Now what?" Benson asked.

"Do as he has done, with your right hand."

At once an Indian moved forward, took the feathered lance from the one who had signalled, and returned to the line. Then the two began to walk their ponies slowly down the hill.

"Do we wait here?" Benson asked.

"No. We go to meet them. Slow. Put your gun away. Keep your hands where they can see them."

"I don't like this," Benson said. "Before we meet we'll be in rifle range. You said they have rifles."

41

"Yes. But what choice do we have? Look at them. They've been on the run, fighting for years. And they outnumber us two to one. And they're hungry. They've got to feed their squaws and little ones stashed away in some canyon. They'll have some of our beef, one way or another. No way can we stop them. We can kill some of them. They can kill some of us. But they'll get food for their families."

That was the longest speech Benson had heard the old scout make. He turned to look at the man riding beside him -- a man he had come to hold in great respect. If there was any fear in his heart, it did not show in his face, as stoic as though he was riding out to check on grass for the cattle. Jan Raphael had referred to him as the real key man for the drive, in this land of unmapped trails. Certainly he was that, and much more.

The Apaches came on, riding with dignity, the little range ponies picking their way carefully down the boulder strewn slope. When they were within twenty paces of Benson and LaRoche, the Chief and his escort pulled up.

The Chief raised his hand. He spoke something in Apache that Benson didn't understand. Benson looked to LaRoche.

"He says they come in peace," LaRoche translated.

"Tell him we also want peace," Benson said. LaRoche interpreted the message.

Again the Chief spoke, his voice low and guttural as he began, and rising to a higher pitch as he continued. He spoke at some length. When he had finished, LaRoche turned to Benson.

"He said the white man has destroyed his people's living. They have killed the buffalo, taking only the hide and leaving the carcass to rot on the prairie. The white man has driven them onto reservations with a promise they would be fed. That has not been so. Their squaws are hungry. Their little ones are starving. They want to barter for beef."

"Barter?" Benson queried. "What do they have to barter?"

Again LaRoche spoke to the Chief. After a brief conversation between

42

the two, he turned to Benson.

"He says he has information about a band of white men who intend to steal the herd. His scouts have followed them as they shadowed the movement of the cattle. He knows where they are holed up in a canyon and where they intend to ambush your men."

"Do you believe him?"

LaRoche was serious. "I do believe him. Even if I didn't, I think handing over a few head peaceably would be much better than having to fight them."

"Ask him how many?"

LaRoche spoke to the Chief. The Chief held up both hands with fingers extended five times.

"Fifty head," LaRoche said.

"Tell him we'll give him forty."

After a brief conversation between the two Indians, the Chief nodded approval.

"Tell him we will expect him to show you where the rustlers are holed up and where they are most likely to plan a surprise."

"He has already promised to do that."

"Do you think he will keep that promise after he gets the cattle?"

"I know he will."

"We'll cut out forty head and drive them across the valley," Benson said. "They can take over there. I'd rather keep them at a distance."

Benson turned back to speak briefly with O'Quinn. Together, with the help of Weaver, they began to cut out longhorns from the drag.

CHAPTER 8

When the riders had abandoned the drive to lend Benson and O'Quinn support in case the Indians attacked, the longhorns had scattered, moving away singly and in small groups. Once the threat of attack was over and the Mascaleros disappeared with their bounty, the riders turned to the task of gathering the longhorns back into a trail herd again.

They moved the cattle only a few miles. By mid evening they had pulled them in close to the banks of the Pecos and let them graze. LaRoche had gone with the Indian scouts to learn the location of the rustler band and to size up the ground where they could expect trouble. If there was a threat of outlaw attack, Benson wanted his report before moving farther. So, once again the drive was stalled. And once again the urgency to get Jan Raphael to a doctor was put on hold.

Weary riders, who had scoured the rough ground to the West, filtered in with strays and fed them into the bed grounds. They slid from their sweat drenched mounts to relax tired muscles and sip scalding coffee.

Hovering in the steam from the large black pots, Skip sniffed the beans and beef and the third pot of coffee since he had kindled an early fire. Time had dulled the light in his ancient eyes but not the bite of his tongue. He snapped and scolded as the riders drifted in to peek into the pots with complaints of hunger, and to fill their tin cups with boiling brew.

"Worse than a pack of kids," Skip grumbled to Benson, who sat on the black stud at the rear of the covered wagon, talking to Jan Raphael. "You'd think they's plumb starved."

"Been a trying day, Skip," Benson smiled. "They're tired and hungry. Hungry enough that even your cooking is going to taste good tonight."

"Drat you, Nathan Benson," Skip snarled as he dipped a bean from the pot with a wooden ladle and tested it between thumb and forefinger. "Drat your ornery hide. You ain't no better'n the rest of em."

He continued to grumble as he mixed batter and drug out live coals to begin the monumental task of baking range biscuits for a pack of hungry trail hands.

Nardi O'Quinn rode in. Benson crossed the stud to where he had dropped rein and stepped from the saddle.

"How many do you think we lost?" Benson asked as he dismounted and lifted a stirrup fender to ease the cinch.

"Only a few. Maybe a dozen, maybe not that many. We scoured the area pretty good, since we're putting the drive on hold. Anyway, not nearly as many as you gave away."

"Didn't exactly give them away. Traded them for information."

"You really think them redskins are going to keep their word?" O'Quinn's voice was filled with sarcasm.

"LaRoche thinks so. Anyway, it was better than a fight. They'd made us pay a price and we'd made them pay a price. And it shouldn't be that way."

Surprise registered behind the red beard. "You ain't going soft on them redskins, are you Benson? I'd made them fight for anything they got."

"We steal their land, kill off their game, then raise hell when they come looking for food for their families. It isn't right."

"They're savages," O'Quinn countered. "Wild, dangerous savages. You've got to treat them that way."

"They're human beings," Benson said.

"Could be you've got some Indian blood in your veins,"

"If I had I'd count it an honor."

"And then it could be you've got a soft spot," O'Quinn said. "If it is, Benson, it'll get you killed some day. I know you're fast, damn fast. Your reputation beat you to Stockton by months. But you've got to be hard, man, hard and mean as all hell if you're going to stay alive as a gunman; even if you're billed as the fastest gun in all of Texas."

"I make no claim to that."

"You don't have to. Your fame outruns you. Soon every kid gunman in the country will be looking for you. Each one hoping by some bit of luck to best you and feather his own cap. You can hang that gun up now, Benson. It isn't too late for you. Don't wait until you're like me, running and fighting, then running to keep from fighting again."

"I've a job to do," Benson said slowly, his eyes trailing out to the south and west -- out to where he had lost the trail of Shack Cumby.

"You think you'll find him?"

"Him?" Benson's eyes flashed to O'Quinn.

"Shack Cumby."

"You know a lot about my business," Benson said.

"I'm a gunman. Knowing about other gunmen helps keep me alive." O'Quinn was silent for a moment. "If you find Cumby," he continued. "Or maybe I should say, when you find him, what do you intend to do?"

"He killed my old man." The words were edged with bitterness. "When I find him I'll put a bullet between his eyes."

"You've a way out, Benson. Why don't you take it?"

"How?"

"Don't tell me you haven't seen the look in Lore Raphael's eyes."

"I've seen it, sure. But that dosen't square my account with Cumby."

"If you've seen it then do something about it man. I had a chance like that once, lots of years back." O'Quinn was staring out across the plain, his expression masked by the red beard. Only his eyes showed the depth of his feeling. "I was young then," he continued. "Young and hot headed. Now I remember it all too well. Remember it each night I lay down with my saddle for a pillow and my gun within arm's reach. Bury that bitterness, Benson, before it's too late."

"After I square with Cumby."

"It may not still be there. Mine wasn't."

"It's a chance I'll have to take."

O'Quinn paused as Lore rode over from the wagon.

"How long you think we'll have to hold up?" she asked Benson. "Dad's not doing any good at all."

"We should be able to get back on the trail tomorrow. I'd like to have LaRoche's report on the outlaws before we move on."

"No matter," said O'Quinn. "They'll try to take us by surprise."

"LaRoche should be back before morning," Benson said. "And we need his report."

A coyote yapped somewhere out on the plains and night came down out of the mountains to engulf the herd in darkness.

CHAPTER 9

Morning came to the low mesas of The Territory, cold and gray. The herd stirred to wakefullness. Already Skip had fed the riders by the light of a great open fire and was stowing his gear in the front of the wagon. The myriad of stars began to blink out as a flare of light climbed up from the eastern horizon.

Benson and O'Quinn stood at the tailgate of the wagon. Jan Raphael peered out of the opened canvas flaps, his face thin and chalky in the flickering light of the fire.

"Don't know the trail myself," Raphael said. His eyes moved anxiously from O'Quinn to Benson. "I was relying completely on LaRoche to guide us through. I had so much faith in his ability to survive, I never thought about losing him."

"I'm of a mind those Apaches did him in yesterday," O'Quinn said. "Don't know why that hard headed old scamp ever went anywhere with them Apaches. Being half Indian himself, he should have known better than to trust them."

"You have any thinking on the trail up ahead?" Raphael spoke to O'Quinn, but he looked out across the plain. The firelight cast shadows in the furrows that seemed to cut deeper into his face each day.

"I started out on one drive," O'Quinn spat at the fire. His eyes held to the red embers that were slowly turning to ash. "We went up the other side of the Pecos. Had some good men and about a thousand steers. We didn't make it."

"Indians?"

"Nope," O'Quinn spat into the fire again. "Comanches jumped us. A small party. We fought them off."

There was silence. Then, O'Quinn spoke slowly, his eyes still on the fire. "We were feeling pretty good about getting past the Comanches. Then we got ambushed by a bunch of rustlers."

"Whew!" Skip said as he tied his bean pot onto the wagon. "That's hard luck. Make it past them Comanch and get bushwhacked by a bunch of scalawags!"

"Must have been twenty or more in that bunch that jumped us," O'Quinn said.

"They catch you with your pants down, did they?" Skip cackled.

"Maybe we just got careless. Only two of us got out. They murdered the rest, killed them on the spot. We hightailed it back the way we came, playing hide and seek with the Comanches. I packed a bullet in my leg. Scoop was the only one who didn't get hit."

"Scoop?" Benson said, surprise registering in his voice. "Scoop Hailey?"

"That's news to me," Raphael said. "Didn't know he had ever been up this way."

"Oh, he's been up this way," O'Quinn spoke with emphasis. "We got separated during the fight. He didn't catch up with me until I was three days down the trail. We hid from Comanches by day and moved by night. Scoop had a gift at finding good places to hide -- wading the river down into the thickets and the like."

"That's good to know," Raphael said. "You think he could guide us if LaRoche doesn't get back?"

"LaRoche will be back," Benson cut in before O'Quinn could answer.

And, almost as if on Benson's command, the old scout walked in out of the shadow, leading his mount. He dropped the reins to ground tie the mare, who stood with sagging head and eyes half closed. LaRochee loosened the cinch, threw off the mare's saddle, and removed her bridle. He dug a tin cup from his saddle roll and filled it with coffee from the camp pot. In true Indian fashion he dropped to the ground with legs crossed under him.

His eyes held to the dying embers of the cook fire as he rolled the cup in his hands, occasionally sipping the steaming brew. He had not spoken, had not looked at anyone.

Raphael looked at Benson -- saw the bewilderment on his face.

"It's a ritual with him," Raphael said. "Something has happened that he's thanking the spirits for, or maybe making atonement for. We'll never know just what. Give him time."

Benson noded thoughtfully, then turned to O'Quinn.

"Roust them out and build the point," Benson said. "Start them north and we'll be along with trail instructions later."

Already riders were working the remuda, roping the horses and dallying their lariats, cutting out mounts for the day. One by one, they threw on the saddles and cinched them tight. Then a rider would swing aboard to buck out the devil that somehow had worked its way down under those mustang skins during the night.

Lore brought grain from the wagon and fed her blue mare. She mounted and rode around to where Benson waited.

Skip drew a bucket of water from the barrell on the side of the wagon and doused the fire. He hitched the team, all the while mumbling to himself. Then he pointed the wagon north. North in the dust of the drag.

Abruptly the old scout stood up and turned to where Benson and Lore waited. He stretched, yawned, and rubbed his eyes.

"Ah," he said, as though he had only then become aware of their presence. "You waitin' for me?"

"You had a long night," Benson stood.

"Very long," LaRoche said.

"What did you learn from the Apaches?"

"Something very good," LaRoche said. "Very good. Without their help, we'd lose half of our men before we knew what hit us."

"Tell me about it," Benson said.

"The Apaches took me right to the rustler's hideout. We took our time closing in on them. Apache scouts move real slow. They didn't want to take a chance on alerting any guards the rustlers might have had out."

"How far up trail?" Benson asked.

"Fifteen, maybe twenty miles. After we pulled out of the rustler's camp, they led me to a cove a few miles this side of where they thought the outlaws would set up their ambush. They suggested we bed the cattle down in that cove after the drive. When we head out the next day, we stampede the herd just before we reach the ambush."

"When you got in close," Benson saked, "could you hear what they were talking about?"

"Some," LaRoche sipped at his coffee. "Mostly gab about cattle. Guessing what they might bring on the market. Some of them talked like they didn't want to go to Sumner. Seems they have some problem with the Cavalry."

"Did they talk about this drive?"

"That was the talk. They're talking like they already have a sure thing. And they would have, if we hadn't been warned."

"Can you describe the location of the suspected ambush so we can plan for it?"

"Better than that," said LaRoche. "I'll take you there tonight after the herd is bedded down. After dark, of course. We want them surprised, not us."

"Any idea how many there are?" Benson asked.

"Two dozen, maybe more. Couldn't tell for sure. They had a big fire and kept coming and going."

"We'll ride ahead to give instructions for the day's drive," said Benson. "Cut out a fresh horse after you have rested a bit. We'll check out the cove so our point doesn't miss it."

"Old Blue'll get me there after she's rested a bit," LaRoche said. "I'll catch you up the line. You just keep the drive moving. We want to reach that cove before dark. And we want them to know we're bedded down there, so they'll get in place for their ambush. We're going to be watched closely today."

CHAPTER 10

When the herd neared the cove Benson was already there, signaling them where to begin the bend. The lead steers swung about with little prodding, and the circle began to form. Gradually it tightened until the outer edge of the opening became a mass of cloven hoofprints. Around and around they milled until they ground to a stop, like a giant wheel that had lost its momentum.

Benson was leading the blue roan. LaRoche had taken to the hills on foot more than an hour earlier. As the bed grounds filled, he came out of a deep crevice looking like a mythical gnome returning from a quest. Benson rode out to meet him, leading LaRoche's blue mare. Once LaRoche was mounted, he motioned with his head westward toward a group of rocky foothills in front of a high mesa.

"Their scouts are up in those rocks," he said. "They're glassing the herd now. They think they have it timed almost to the minute when we'll pass their ambush. They're probably feeling pretty cocky right about now."

"Maybe we can relieve them of some of that feeling soon," Benson said. "We'd probably have lost the herd tomorrow without the help of the Apaches."

"You understand," LaRoche said. "The Apaches are only people, just like my people, the Crow. And they're not bad, as some would have you believe. The day will come when the world will see my people in a different light."

As darkness settled in, LaRoche and Benson rode out into the night. About four miles ahead they came to a place where the valley narrowed, with steep hills on either side.

"You see," LaRoche said, "with men placed up in the rocks on both sides, they could empty many saddles with one volley. What we want is to place a couple of good men where they can see the outlaws when they come out of cover."

"A good idea," Benson said. "They'll not expect a stampede. When they realize what's happening, they'll have to make a break for their horses."

About a hundred yards before the pass they found a clump of grease-wood where two men could conceal themselves and be above the path of the herd. Still, if the longhorns spread wide, they could well crash through the greasewood clump. They selected a spot among the rocks higher up. It would be a longer shot, but safer.

Satisfied with their reconnaissance, they turned back to select the point where the stampede would be started. The moon had now come up and they studied the trail as they returned.

With the riders gathered around the fire, Benson laid out the action for the following day in the same manner that he might have planned a charge of the light cavalry at Petersburg. Weary riders, who had heard the horror stories of outlaws who plagued the Chisholm Trail, listened intently. They were aware that not only the herd, but their own lives were at stake.

At the big bend of the river, about four miles up, they would start the stampede. The right flank guards and the point would swing left and the cattle would be turned north just beyond the bend. That would point them at the pass. Any rustlers caught on the right of the pass would be unable to join the gang until the longhorns passed. Hopefully, Wellman and Buttons, hidden on the left rise, could pick off some of the outlaws on that side. Any way they could cut down the number of the attackers would help. For, according to LaRoche's estimate, the trail riders would be badly outnumbered.

The cattle were thrown on the trail with the break of day. Already Wellman and Buttons had taken up their positions near the pass, having hidden their mounts in an arroyo directly behind them.

O'Quinn and Donnel built the point. Buell, riding a fleet little cowpony, took up position on the right flank. Once the longhorns were pointed toward the pass, he was to quarter across the face of the stampede, dropping back to join the fight. Anxious riders cast furtive glances to the rocky hills west and urged the cattle along.

Riding the west rim of the herd, Benson drew his six-gun at the point where the stampede was to begin. He fired two quick shots into the grayness of the early morning.

A nearby steer lifted his long horns and rolled his frightened eyes until the whites showed. With a bellow he was off. Another followed, then another. Soon, there were a hundred steers in mad flight. Long horns clashed. Sharp tines ripped. Fright flowed across the herd like a storm wave on the ocean. Now five hundred head. Now a thousand. Then half that number again. All thundering across the valley with only one purpose in mind -- to run. They did not know where. Just run.

Riders shouted in high pitched tones that were lost in the pounding of hooves, the rattle of horns, the hoarse bellow of frightened cattle.

Benson sent the stud along the left flank, following LaRoche. Dust lifted in a billowy cloud. Caught in the down draft, the dust filtered south to choke his lungs and blur his vision. In the melee he thought of Lore. He hoped she was on the far side of the herd and that the fight would be over before she could drop around the drag. He caught his hand firming up on the reins to pull up. Then he set his jaw. He touched spurs to his mount's flanks and sent him racing past the fleeing cattle.

Out ahead O'Quinn and Donnel were beginning the turn, hazing the point, riding dangerously close to the waving horns of the maddened herd. Gradually, the long line gave way, swinging north. North toward the pass.

Weaver was on the bend, riding in, beating at the steers with his rope. Behind him came Benson and LaRoche. Farther back, Tarp Dailey came out of the dust, his pony racing ahead.

The flank steers crowded in, straightening the bend. Benson watched LaRoche. He saw the scout turn away from the rim and swing north of west. He lifted a hand to Dailey. Dailey and LaRoche fell away and followed. Out ahead O'Quinn and Donnel pulled up and dropped in behind the scout. Weaver saw what was happening and swung out to join them.

Benson's stud, Partner, was pounding along at an easy lope now, and Benson dropped his knotted reins over the saddle horn. He drew cartridges from his vest pocket and reloaded his six-gun. Then he loosened the lashings from the saddle boot and drew the carbine. He levered a shell into the chamber and let the rifle rest across the pommel of the saddle.

The stampede was rolling along like a loaded freight train at full throttle. Benson lifted a hand and bellowed into the new day. The riders pulled down to an easy lope, saving their mounts, preparing for the hard run they could anticipate on the trail ahead.

Quartering away from the herd, LaRoche was hardly five hundred yards from the arroyo when he heard three rapid shots. They were fired from a rocky point far to the west, too far away to have been intended for Benson and his men. Evidently the shots were a prearranged signal. What the signal signified, they could only guess.

Out ahead Wellman and Buttons heard the shots. Earlier, in the predawn light, they had watched a dozen rustlers split up, taking cover on both sides of the narrow pass. They had held their fire rather than give their position away. Immediately following the signal, they saw the twelve outlaws come out of their cover, racing for horses they had tethered at the far end of the pass.

Wellman fired two quick shots. One of the outlaws went down. Another stopped to help him. He threw up his hands and toppled over backward when Button's rifle spoke. The others were stooped low now, darting from cover to cover, making difficult targets of themselves. They did not take time to see where the shots were coming from, or make any attempt to return the fire.

Wellman and Buttons each fired again, with no apparent hits. Then they came out of their cover and raced for their own horses. They had hardly reached the trail riders when a wave of outlaws came from behind the hill above the pass and cantered down the slope, firing wildly.

Benson shifted forward in the saddle. He felt the stud break away. Out ahead he saw LaRoche lift his rifle over his head, splitting the morning with the war cry of his Crow ancestors.

Off to the right, riding the rim of the fleeing cattle, O'Quinn drew his rifle and fired the first shot. He watched a rustler go down and lifted his red bearded face to the sky, letting loose a wild Rebel yell.

The surprised rustlers, expecting to find the trail riders scattered, wheeled away and circled wide, firing as they rode. There were now more than a dozen of them, and still they came, a steady stream of mounted, armed men. Desperate men, willing to take desperate chances to get what they wanted.

Like a cornered checker player, Benson had known all along that he could not trade man for man.

"Take cover," he shouted. Riders spilled from their saddles, seeking cover behind rocks and in depressions -- all, that is, except O'Quinn. He was racing his mount back and forth, making a moving target of himself, yelling like a Comanche warrior.

The rustlers scattered, but not soon enough. From their stationary positions, the trail riders' shots began to connect. Already three riderless outlaw horses quartered back across the slope. But at the same time, their numbers were growing. The ten who escaped from the pass now joined the attack.

A small group of outlaws rode out the ridge, drawing down toward the tail end of the herd. Possibly, Benson reasoned, they intended to circle the stationary trail riders when the stampede had passed.

But there was little he could do about it at the present. What he needed was for his men to empty more saddles. And he needed those other riders caught on the right flank.

Simpson, coming out of the drag, was caught in a burst of fire from the rustlers just above him and knocked from his mount. Before he got to his feet a second volley slammed him to the ground. He lay still. Benson logged up the first casualty for his men. He saw one outlaw keeping back up from the others, apparently directing the attack. The man probably thought he was out of rifle range, but Benson's first shot doubled him up. A second sent him flying from the saddle.

Two of the rustlers appeared to have given up the fight. They were racing back along the flank of the herd, moving away from the fight. Then, with horror, Benson saw Lore ride out from the drag. He leaped for his mount, realizing even as he moved, that he was too late. Already O'Quinn was racing down the flank of the herd, riding low in the saddle. And his big blood bay was at a dead run.

Lore saw the men, knew their intent. She threw up her rifle and emptied one saddle. But O'Quinn had moved into her line of fire, and she was afraid to shoot again. The other rustler was coming on. He wanted that woman, and he was willing to gamble his life for her. She wheeled and raced away, but her pursuer was on a faster horse. When she looked back, she could see that he was gaining.

Up above, a group of four outlaws swung down to cut off any of the trail riders from rescuing the woman. Just like their comrade, they wanted her--wanted her almost as much as they wanted the cattle. They waited until O'Quinn was directly below them and they all fired at once.

The bay had been gaining, but no longer. He was hit by more than one round and went down. O'Quinn went spinning on the ground. He came up, his left arm dangling. He had lost his rifle but he raced to the downed horse and took cover behind him. He drew his six-gun, cursing as the hammer fell on a spent catridge.

It was then that little Kenny Wiggins, the timid kid from El Paso, came up from behind. He saw what was happening and turned his mount straight up the slope, directly toward the four charging outlaws. He fired, and a rustler horse went down. But the three others pulled up, taking careful aim. There were three simultaneous shots. Little Kenny Wiggins went back over the rump of his horse and lay still.

One outlaw, whose horse had been shot out from under him by Kenny, raced for Kenny's mount. But LaRoche, with his rifle supported on a rock, took aim. It was a long shot but the .50 caliber was a long range gun. An instant after the big gun roared, the rustler staggered forward, tumbling down the hill.

Benson raced the stud back along the flank of the cattle. But now he saw the futility of his effort. The three outlaws who had murdered Kenny Wiggins had him cut off. Others were joining them. Getting himself killed would not help Lore, though the thought of the fate that awaited her back at the rustler hangout sent cold chills racing through his body. If he was to find her, if he was to rescue her, he had to stay alive. He pulled up, dismounted, and hit the gound again. He found cover, and the fired at the outlaws with a deadly thirst for vengeance.

But now, another rider came on the scene. Like a shadow he came -- out of a deep ravine. His bare legs gripped the sides of his fleet range pony. There was no saddle to add weight to his mount. Nor was there a heavy weapon, only a long feathered lance. An eagle feather dangled from his hair. And with the grace and ease of one long accustomed to battle, he swept out onto the field of battle. Like his rider, the little range pony was no stranger to war. When the chief leaned forward and spoke into the pony's ear, he doubled his speed. Perhaps he knew that speed was what had kept him and his master alive in those other battles. Perhaps there was a rapport between the pony and his rider that no one could explain.

Too late, the rustler saw the nose of the Indian pony creep up beside him. Too late, he drew his gun, throwing a shot wildly back over his shoulder. Too late, a flint tipped lance buried itself in the rustler's back, driving forcefully through his lungs and heart. Too late, and another riderless horse quartered out across the plain.

The Apache Chief turned his mount. He lifted his feathered lance high and an Apache war whoop rang across the plain. As if in answer, a series of whoops rose from the hill crest in back of the outlaws. A dozen braves swept over the hill. A dozen more, and still they came. A few fired their ancient rifles, while the others rained arrows down on the outlaws.

Caught between the trail riders and the Indian warriors, the rustlers turned tail, fleeing the slaughter with all the speed they could muster out of their mounts. But on the hillside, they left more dead than they had ever dreamed possible.

The Apaches pulled up short of the trail riders. The Chief joined them. He lifted his right hand to Benson. Then, as quickly as they had come, they were gone, vanishing over the rise like shadows into the rocks.

The trail riders sat in awed wonder at the silence that had settled about them. The rustlers were gone. The war cry of the Apache and the boom of the guns were stilled. Even the noise of the stampede had faded up the trail. And Lore Raphael, now riding back to join the trail riders, could see from a distance, the look of relief on the hardened face of Benson as he spied her coming up the trail, and knew that she was safe.

CHAPTER 11

On the banks of the Pecos, they milled the herd as twilight sifted down over the plains. Skip had arrived ahead of the cattle; his cook fire glowed a few hundred yards short of the river. He cursed in a brittle voice as he searched for his gear in the front of the wagon in deepening shadows.

After the battle, they had rounded up the longhorns as rapidly as possible and threw them on the trail. Cattle that had strayed too far were left behind. Under constant pressure from Benson, the drive rolled on.

Weary riders prodded weary cattle over the dry and dusty trail. The trail riders turned often in the saddle to study the trail that unrolled slowly behind them -- out to the horizon -- beyond the dust cloud kicked up by the multitude of cloven hooves. Yet all they had seen in the course of the day was an old man slumped on a smoke blue mare, drifting along like a shadow in the wake of the herd.

As Donnel and Weaver swung the point, O'Quinn and Buell moved up to put pressure on the bend. The right flank guards dropped back and the cattle were settled in to graze and water while the riders ate.

O'Quinn, his splinted arm tied to his waist, had ridden flank all day. Benson drifted by, followed by Lore.

"How's the arm?" he asked.

"I've had worse," O'Quinn said.

"Sorry about your horse," Lore said. "I see you found another big bay in the remuda. How's he carrying you?"

"Doing good, but I do miss Big Red."

"The moon will be up in a couple hours," Benson said. "We'll cross in its light. You can help bring up the drag."

"Night crossings can be trouble," O'Quinn said.

"You know we've got to move on," Benson said.

"I know," said O'Quinn. "I'll have to agree with you on this one. But I won't ride in the rear. I'll be right up front with you."

"There's a good chance for problems in any crossing," Benson said. "much less at night. But if anyone out there thinks we're bedding down here, they will expect us to be here come morning. We won't be."

Benson swung the stud about and rode with Lore to the bank of the Pecos.

"Must have had heavy rain farther up," Lore said as they looked out over the muddy stream.

"It's up and it's fast. Lots of mud and floating wood. Not ideal for night crossing."

"Maybe it would be better to wait until morning." Lore's voice registered concern. "We've already lost too many men today."

"We'll cross tonight. Then if we have to run when daylight comes, we can point them north and let them run."

"I hope we don't have to," she said. "They're on the prod, edgy from so much running. They'll stampede at just about any excuse."

"Maybe we won't have to. That's Comanche land over there. And those outlaws were taught a lesson of respect by the Apaches today."

"The rustlers didn't show up this afternoon as we thought they might," Lore said. "Do you suppose they may have given up?"

"Not likely. LaRoche thinks they're still on our trail. I'd say he's right. He figures they'd have tackled us already if it hadn't been for their fear of the Indians. They're just waiting for us to get out of Apache territory."

"Where is he now?" Lore asked.

"Scouting the other bank."

"That poor man." Lore's voice was soft, filled with that strange feminine quality that caused Benson to think of his mother each time he heard it. "He hasn't slept in two days."

"I know," Benson said. "But he wanted a look-see up the other side. Said if there were Indians out there, they would have fires. The Comanches are strong. They're fearless on their own range."

"His mare must be exhausted."

"Completely. He's letting her rest. Took a fresh horse. But I'll wager he'll be riding that blue mare during the crossing."

"Benson." Lore's voice was soft, strained. She turned in the saddle to face him. "LaRoche tells me we'll reach Fort Sumner in a little over a week if we allow grazing time -- sooner if we push them."

"You sound as if you were sorry," There was a question in his voice.

"Oh," Lore said. "I'll be happy enough to get the cattle through, get Dad to a doctor."

"It's been a long hard drive," Benson said. "All the more so because of your Dad's condition."

Her face, copper tanned and wide eyed was upturned to him. "But when the drive is through you'll be leaving?"

"When the drive reaches Fort Sumner my contract with Jan Raphael ends." He met her clear, questioning eyes but had trouble holding them.

"And then you're leaving?" she asked.

"I've got a job to finish." Unconsciously he turned and his eyes trailed out to the south and west -- out across the plains where the shades of night were coming in fast.

"Yes," he said at last. "I'll be leaving."

"I wish you wouldn't."

"It's best," he said. "Best for both of us. You know what I am and I know what I'm not. Neither is good for you."

Lore leaned over. She removed a skin-tight riding glove and placed a soft hand on his. "Yes. I know what you are. But I like what I've seen, and I know what I want."

She paused a moment, reading what was so visible in his face before she continued. "Ride back to the ranch with us. There's a place there for you, permanent."

Benson had faced up to nine men in a fight to the death. He had ridden to defeat with the ragged, determined cavalry of Fritz Lee in the Army of Northern Virginia. He had heard the whine of hot lead and felt its stab. Yet never had he experienced the combined feeling of fright, coupled with exhilaration that flashed through his body at the touch of Lore Raphael's hand.

He wanted to draw back. Wanted to run away from this strange circumstance that threatened to engulf him and shatter his quest, to make a mockery of his years of weary search. Where dwelt the man who would not jump at the opportunity to ride home with this fascinating product of the Texas plains?

Still, there was his vow of vengeance. There was that obligation to repay, which had awaited him that day when he returned from one bitter defeat, only to face another of much greater personal magnitude.

The battle Benson now fought within himself was greater than any he could ever fight with Shack Cumby. He had been aware of the invisible struggle for days. Until this moment, he was certain he would win. Suddenly, he wasn't so sure.

The clang of Skip's spoon-in-a-pan brought them about. Lore withdrew her hand and slid it back into her glove, but her eyes had not left Benson's. Perhaps she was seeing in his face, in his expression, the things he could not find words to say -- maybe was afraid to admit. She smiled.

"Let's see if Skip's beef is fit to eat," she said. "We may need it before the night is over."

"May be a long night," Benson said as they turned and rode toward the wagon. But his mind was not on the night crossing -- the flooded river--the outlaws back there on the trail. His mind was on the one thing that the code of the west demanded he do for Saul Benson. In direct conflict to that, was the longing that had been building inside him since he first met this woman with hair the color of a raven's wing, and eyes that sparkled like dew in the early morning sun. Those opposing forces were like the jaws of a great vice that was tearing away at his innermost being.

"Yes," Lore said. "It may be a long night."

As she spoke, the muffled rumble of distant thunder rolled down from the north. And far up the Pecos, barely visible above the distant horizon, a billow of storm clouds began to grow.

CHAPTER 12

A wide moon rose out of the east like a great golden disc. It splashed pale yellow light on the plains, and glittered and glimmered from a thousand tiny wavelets on the raging Pecos. In its dull glow O'Quinn and Donnel teased out the lead steers. While Donnel and Dailey fed cattle into the point, O'Quinn threw his mount in the river ahead of the longhorns and pointed him to the far bank. The steers, taking courage from the horse, plunged in and followed close. Fighting the swift current, they headed for the far bank, where Weaver and Hagerman waited to haze them onto the bed grounds.

But many of the steers were weary from the long day's trek. They moved only when prodded along.

"Crowd them in," Benson shouted as a stubborn group began to mill on the bank, trying to turn back against the wave that was building behind them.

The cowmen's cries rose from both sides of the herd as Buttons and Dailey crowded one flank, while Benson and Lore brought up the other. Weary old LaRoche, back from his scouting foray, had pressed his blue mare back in service. He hurried the steers along with a limb he had cut from a cottonwood by the river bank. Even Scoop Hailey and Skip Bonner were riding herd on the rear, helping Wellman and Buell contain the edgy steers, hazing them in, pointing them back toward the river as they tried to break away.

Those head that balked on the bank were driven forward by the weight of the herd. They plunged in and swam for the far bank, following the leaders, fighting the swift current.

A hundred head spilled into the river. Then another hundred. Still they came. A gentle curve began to form in the long line that stretched from bank to bank. The curve deepened as steers yielded to the pressure of the current, threatening to break and send a great wave of longhorns sweeping down the flooded stream.

O'Quinn threw his mount back into the river. Benson swam the black stud along the flank, shouting, beating at the longhorned beasts, forcing them to swim against the current. Behind him Lore rode into the flood, hazing the flank steers, forcing them back, tightening the belly of the curve.

"Throw them in!" Benson shouted as the men on the bank slowed their push to lighten the weight on the bend. "Throw them in the river!"

Again the shouts of night riders lifted from the darkness and floated across the plains, a new cry to this wild and untamed wilderness.

"Throw them in!" and again they came. "Yip, yip, yi. Git dogie, git!"

Half a thousand head had spilled over the bank. Still they came, faster, as pressure built from the rider's effort.

"Whoopee!" LaRoche flailed with his club as he rode.

The peals of thunder, that earlier in the evening had been faint and far away, were now upon them. Long arms of jagged lightning flashed down from the heavens. Storm clouds that were only specks on the northern horizon at nightfall, were now whirling black masses galloping across the sky, blotting out the moon and darkening the night. The wind lifted, shrill through the timber on the river bank. The storm came in with the force and speed of an ocean gale.

Thunder roiled across the plains, crashing against the banks of the Pecos. Lightning played its forked tongues in the tops of the tall cottonwoods. Riders, caught unprepared for the sudden deluge, were drenched by the slashing curtains of rain.

In the sudden darkness and blinding rain, even the cattle did not see the Indian canoe until it was upon them. Hewn from the butt cut of a giant ponderosa, waterlogged and heavy, it had been swept from its mooring somewhere upstream. It plunged along with the current. Though almost fifteen feet from stem to stern, it barely broke the crest. The cattle in its path tried to turn, but there wasn't time. The river was choked with frantic steers, each fighting his own battle with the current. Those ahead were driven along by the mass.

The canoe rammed a steer in the shoulder and spun it around, pointing it downstream. It crashed on, catching another and another, cutting a path through the swimming line and carrying the severed herd down-current with it.

Swimming with the flow of the cattle, Lore saw the line bulge in back of Benson. She threw her mount in below the steers, beating at their faces with her rope. Then the canoe came through. It caught another steer on the neck and spun it about. A longhorn swept down the back of the red roan. It struck Lore in her rib section below the breasts, ripping through her shirt and flesh and throwing her from the saddle.

The canoe lurched on, its speed unchecked. It shot past the last steer and struck the red roan a crushing blow that spun him in the water. When Benson looked back, the roan was on his side, with his rider nowhere in sight.

The red roan righted himself and turned downstream, fighting to outdistance the wave of steers following close behind. Only a few feet ahead of the horse, floundering in the mad swirl, Lore fought to stay above the yellow flood crest.

Benson shouted at the black stud and sent him back toward the break. His gun was out, flaming in the night. Behind him O'Quinn cursed as he urged his big bay through the muddy swirl.

A flare of lightning split the sky as if to open up the very heavens. It played on the longhorns riding the current. For an instant, it revealed Lore, her head above the current, struggling to keep ahead of the cattle. Only a moment and all was black again. The next flash, farther away, revealed the gap between the woman and the steers closing fast.

On the near side of the river Tram Donnel raced his mount to the bank and threw him in, hoping that the momentum would sweep him down past the steers. Yet he was more than thirty feet from the floundering girl when his horse bogged down to a steady swim.

Benson leaned forward, shouting into Partner's ears, laid back along his black neck. For a moment the magnificent animal's feet found bottom. He bunched the muscles of his square, powerful rump and lunged out. Shooting through the water at teriffic speed, he cut in ahead of the lead steers by inches.

Blinded by the last flash of lightning, Benson had lost sight of Lore. Yet the rapport that the man and his mount had established in their years together was at work. The stud read well his rider's intent. Without a cue, he turned down and his legs churned the silt-ladened waters into foam as he swept past the swimming girl.

Benson leaned from the saddle. He circled an arm about Lore's slender waist. He lifted up, pulling her in until she could reach the saddle horn. Still holding onto her lest she lose her hold, he looked about for an avenue of escape. There was none.

Leaderless and frantic, the steers had spread out across the river. Now they were swimming with the current. Their range hardened bodies were forging through the water at amazing speed. Benson attempted to angle across ahead of them. But the additional weight was slowing the stud. He was losing ground fast. Their only chance was to swim with the current. Yet, even there they were fighting a losing battle.

Donnel urged his mount in against the flank, trying to bend the line and give Benson an opening. He reached the lead steers and moved in. Closer and closer he crowded. Beating at their faces, shouting, cursing. A steer lifted his head with the rise of the current. A longhorn lashed out. It caught the man's side, ripping through jacket and flesh. Still he crowded in.

The black stud was hardly five feet in the lead now. Donnel rode in. He drew his six-gun and leaned from the saddle. He shot a steer between and just above the eyes. Then another and another. He emptied his gun. Six steers floated with the pace of the river, heads down, no longer forging ahead by their own effort. Others beside them gave way. The line began to bend. Slowly at first, but it bent.

By now Dailey had thrown his mount in and was backing Donnel up. Then came LaRoche. He pressed his mare along the flank, rapping steers with his club, whooping above the roar of the river. They formed a wall, boring in, crowding the steers. Gradually the line turned and swung toward the far bank.

Seeing the opening, Benson turned right. He came out of the river and up the steep bank.

By now the storm was over. It had dashed in suddenly. It dashed out in the same manner. And once again the moon looked down on the Pecos.

On the bank Benson eased Lore down. She stood leaning against the stud, exhausted.

"You're hurt," he said and his voice was heavy with fear.

"Only scratched," she said. "And winded a little. I couldn't see you, but I knew those longhorns were close. I guess I was swimming pretty hard."

Benson leaned down, caught her and pulled her around. He drew a heavy breath as he saw the bloodstain spreading down the front of her shirt.

"You're hurt," he said again. "Bad hurt." He leaped down from Partner and, lifting her up, he placed her in the saddle.

"Go back to the wagon," he demanded. His hand, lingering momentarily on her waist, trembled a bit. His face was ashen in the moonlight. "I'll send Skip back to doctor that wound."

"Do you think I'm going off and leave you here afoot with all those frightened longhorns around?"

"Your horse came ashore a little ways down. I'll get him and help finish the crossing. Then I'll see you back at the wagon."

"I'll go to the wagon when the steers are on the other side," she said firmly. And even as she spoke she wheeled the stud and drove back into the river.

CHAPTER 13

Daylight found the herd trailing north. North through the wild land of the Comanche. Trailing up the Pecos on the last leg of the journey to Fort Sumner. After crossing the Pecos last night, they had moved the cattle out by moonlight. They bedded them down almost a mile from the river. Then, this morning they had thrown them on the trail more than an hour before daylight.

LaRoche sat slumped in the saddle. One might have thought he was sleeping, but he wasn't. For the whole of that pre-dawn hour he had watched the riders working -- watched the cattle swing into that long tireless stride that could eat up twenty miles a day and still allow for grazing time. Now with daylight, he watched the back trail for the outlaws.

Benson and O'Quinn were planning the day when LaRoche rode over to them.

"About five or six miles up you will find a cove that reaches out to the right," LaRoche told O'Quinn. "Out away from the river. Good grass. Well protected. Drive there and wait for us. No bad water in that valley."

LaRoche pulled his mount about and rode off.

"We're going back to the crossing," Benson said. "Try to bluff off the outlaws -- if they come. And we think they will. If we don't catch you by noon you'll know something went wrong. Move them on and do your best."

Benson swung around and followed LaRoche.

They rode back to the wagon where Skip had already killed the fire and loaded his gear. He was now perched on the wagon seat with the lines in his hands. As usual, he grumbled to himself as he waited for orders to move out -- impatient to be out and away.

Lore climbed down from the wagon as they rode up. "How's your scratch this morning?" Benson asked.

"A little sore," she smiled. "With another application of Skip's firewater

I'll be as good as new -- if it doesn't burn a hole right through me."

"I thought I told you to ride the wagon today," Benson said. "Why is your roan saddled up?"

Lore flipped the loose strands of her hair back from her face, laughing softly. "I thought we went over this last night," she said, as she gathered the reins to her mount and walked away from the wagon.

Benson stepped down from his saddle. Trailing the stud, he walked along beside her.

"I haven't forgotten last night," he said. "I'll be keeping a little closer check on my mount today. I don't want to be left walking again."

They both laughed. When they were out of hearing range from the wagon, Lore became serious.

"I'm worried," she said, then paused as she turned to face Benson. "Dad isn't doing any good at all. In fact, he's worse. He's losing ground fast. I didn't realize just how fast until last night."

"Is the infection in the wound worse?"

"Yes. It's deep. Skip says he can't get to it. That's why he is so impatient. He says we need a doctor, and soon."

Benson stared out the broad trail where the herd had now disppeared.

"We're a long ways from a doctor," he said. "I talked with LaRoche this morning. He thinks we're at least six days out of Sumner. That's if we push hard and don't run into any more trouble."

"And just what are the chances of more trouble?" Lore asked.

"If we can shake the outlaws back at the crossing, we'll be through with them. This is Comanche land. They won't follow us here. But getting the cattle past the Comanches may be a serious problem. When we get close to Fort Sumner we'll likely have outlaws to deal with again -- and we won't have the Apaches to rescue us."

"Do you think it might be possible to send the wagon on ahead and get Dad to a doctor quicker?"

"Let's talk to LaRoche," Benson said. He signalled and the scout rode out to them.

When Lore asked LaRoche about sending the wagon ahead, the expression on the old scout's face never changed. He looked intently at Lore for a moment, while he pondered a decision that would violate his better judgment. He turned himself in the saddle to face north. Lifting a long arm he swung it east and then north.

"All this is Comanche land." he said. "We may get through, but only if we stay together. At that we'll have to hide and run--maybe fight if we don't hide well."

"Then you see no chance?" Lore asked.

"No chance at all."

Lore looked back at the wagon.

"Then all I know to do is get the drive through as fast as possible," she said.

"We'll do our best to shove them through," Benson said. "But right now we'd better get that wagon moving before we have company from across the river."

"I'll send Skip out." Lore stepped into the saddle and pulled her mount about. "The two of you plan to take on the whole outlaw gang?"

"We'll just give them a warm reception at the crossing."

"I hope you know what you're doing."

Benson looked at LaRoche and smiled. "The scout here thinks he does. Me, I hope he's right."

LaRoche rode back along the broad trail left by the herd. Benson swung up and followed.

A hundred yards short of the crossing, LaRoche pulled up. He motioned Benson to do likewise. They tied their mounts in a thicket and went ahead on foot. The scout moved with the stealth of a fox. Benson tried to imitate him.

Just above the beaten trail, Benson hid in a clump of alders, settling in so he would be well concealed, yet have a clear view of the far river bank.

"They'll probably have scouts out when they come," LaRoche said. "After yesterday, they'll be a mite more cautious."

"I hope we can give them another surprise," Benson said.

"Let them get all the way to the river," LaRoche said. "Fire when I do. Three shots with your rifle, then empty your short gun. Throw lead as fast as you can. We want them to think there are several of us. Shoot fast, but make your shots count if you can. If we can drop two or three of them, it will give them more reason to skedaddle."

The scout surveyed the plain across the river.

"We're just in time," he said. "I just saw one of them darting for cover."

He was on foot. Once they see the cattle are gone, they'll come on fast."

"Let's hope this works," Benson said.

"It'll work," LaRoche said, as he flattened himself on the ground. He crawled across to the other side of the herd's path like an overgrown serpent. Within seconds he was lost in the growth on the river bank. No movement. Not even a grass blade moved.

The air was still, the morning hushed, only an occasional chirp from a bird in the bush. With LaRoche vanished so completely, Benson was left with a feeling of aloneness. He drew his pistol and lay it within close reach. He placed a handful of cartridges on the ground beside him so he could reload fast. Then he knotted his left fist and thrust it forward, resting the rifle on it with the sights lined on the far bank.

LaRoche was an old hand at the game of scouting. His canny old brain had long ago learned to predict the antics of man. That was what had kept him alive through many clashes on the plains. And once again he had guessed the actions of the outlaws -- guessed them well. For when the scouts discovered that the herd was gone and saw the broad trail leading away on the other side, they signaled their comrades.

Almost at once the gang put their mounts to a hard run and loped up to the river bank. They had brought along the two scouts' horses, and soon all of them were mounted. They paused before the river. Benson could hear a heated discussion. Some of the rustlers wanted to charge on ahead and catch up with the drive before they got too deep into Comanche territory. Others cautioned that they had lost the element of surprise.

One said, "Suppose our gunfire brings on a war party of Comanches? We don't want a repeat of yesterday."

Benson watched the rustlers with growing apprehension. What if LaRoche was wrong? What if, rather than run, they spread out and crossed the Pecos? He and LaRoche would not have a ghost of a chance of getting to their own mounts.

The sun was up now, swinging across the sky, burning down on the plains. And Benson burned with impatience as he waited for LaRoche to commence firing. He felt it would be best to try to turn them before they started crossing. It seemed the old scout felt differently. Or maybe he was hoping that they would turn back on their own.

Benson's hand was wet where he held the gun. Beads of sweat trickled down his forehead. A deerfly began to drill a hole in his chin, but he did not move. He tried to make a hasty count but they were bunched too closely together. He was certain there were more than a dozen -- maybe as many as fifteen.

As the two leaders of the outlaw band stepped their mounts into the water, LaRoche's big Sharps .50 caliber resounded with a deafening roar. The foremost rider was slammed back in the saddle, sliding from his horse into the water. Benson squeezed off three quick shots with his rifle and grabbed for his sixgun.

LaRoche was firing his short gun now and letting out a series of war whoops that sounded like an entire party of Crow Warriors were cached away in the bushes there on the river bank. Benson joined in with a Rebel yell, throwing his voice first one way and then the other. All the while he was firing wildly with his .44.

The whine of lead, the crash of rifles, the Rebel yell. It brought back bad memories to Benson. Memories of fallen comrades, of bitter defeat. Yet this was something that had to be done. It was the savagery of this wild and untamed land, a land that knew no law other than the law of might. And he was fighting for more than his personal survival, more than a herd of cattle. He was fighting for a woman with hair the color of the raven's wing and dark eyes that sparkled like dew in the early morning sun.

LaRoche's first shot had stopped the gang cold. Then, as Benson had emptied two more saddles, they turned as of one accord. For a moment it seemed that they were going to disperse on the far bank, as they spread out briefly.

Benson dropped his short gun and took up the rifle. He emptied a fourth saddle as LaRoche let out with a weird cry that sounded like a Banshee death knell. That was all it took.

Almost as one, the entire gang put their mounts to a dead run on the back trail, their steel shod hooves kicking up a dust cloud on the hard earth that had already swallowed up the rain of last night. They had not seen one target -- had not fired one shot. But they knew that four horses with empty saddles were galloping along behind them.

Benson stood up to get a clear view. When his final shot rang out he saw a rider slump forward in the saddle. But he was still up, clinging to the saddle horn, when they rode out of sight.

Then there was silence -- deathly silence. The furious firing had stilled even the birds. Benson lowered his rifle. He could feel the warm barrel and smell the odor of burnt powder. Methodically, almost without thought, he drew shells from his vest pockets and began to feed them into his guns.

LaRoche remained in his cover for several minutes before he came out in a crouched position. He motioned Benson to follow, and they set off toward their horses, hitting a brisk pace. They kept out of the trail, holding to the cover of weeds and brush.

They reached their horses, mounted and rode in against the river until they were close to a mile upstream. Then they turned east and put their mounts to a fast lope until they cut across the trail of the herd. LaRoche pulled his mare down to a gentle rolling pace. It was a gait she could hold for hours while her rider slumped in the saddle, his body swaying with the motion of the animal beneath him.

A soft breeze came up from the river. It wafted across the plain, taking some of the bite out of the sun. Benson pulled his mount down and rode abreast of the scout -- following the broad trail until they overtook the herd.

Already O'Quinn had found the cove. The longhorns were scattered across the plain, feeding on clumps of buffalo grass. Riders moved in a wide circle around the herd, hazing back strays.

LaRoche pulled up by the wagon. Skip had placed the wagon near a thicket of scrub brush and was gathering wood.

"No fires today," the old scout cautioned. "Comanches can see smoke in daylight from far off."

He addressed himself to Benson but his eyes were on the wood.

"Okay! Okay!" Skip mumbled with audible irritation. "I ain't no green-horn, you know."

LaRoche ignored the comment. He sat for a moment in silence. His eyes swept the landscape to the north like a falcon looking for prey. He lifted his long arm and pointed up the Pecos.

"I'll scout out the trail," he said simply. "Hold the herd. I'll be back."

He loosed his reins, shifted forward in the saddle, and the blue mare hit a steady rolling pace north.

Benson watched him ride away. Then, he turned the stud out to the rim of the herd. Lore was taking a turn at day guard, moving slowly among the grazing steers, singing a soft ballad as she rode.

"I'll bet your mother taught you that song," he said as he rode up.

She half turned, looked at him for a long moment.

"No," she said. "Dad sang that to me when I was a girl. In fact, that was the first song I can remember him singing. I think that's why I like it so much."

"Your mother," Benson said. "I've never heard you talk about her."

"No," she said. "No, you haven't. I leave that to the past. I think it's better that way."

"I'm sorry," he said.

"Don't be. I want you to know. Mom was a dance hall girl. That is, the only mother I ever knew. She left Dad about a year after he brought me in. I was only four or five then and can't remember much about her. Only that she didn't care for me. And she let me know it when Dad wasn't around."

"I'm sorry again."

"I'm not. Dad gave me enough love and care for two parents. He raised me himself. No grandparents. No uncles or aunts. No help from anyone," she smiled and lifted a hand to brush back strands of hair from her face, "And he taught me to ride and shoot rather than cook and sew. I like it that way."

"You said Jan brought you in?" Benson's voice was puzzled. "From where?"

"He was returning from a cattle buying trip back east. He found me wandering along the trail just south of Waco. It was somewhere near Lorena. That's why he named me Lorena."

"Then you don't know who your real parents were?"

"No. I haven't the slightest idea. All I can remember was like a bad dream. I was hiding. There were guns firing and I was frightened. I have no idea who was doing the shooting. I've always felt that, whoever they were, they killed my folks."

"Did he try to find your people?"

"Yes. He inquired along the way and got no clue. He caught up with two wagon trains but I didn't belong in either one. I think he was glad he didn't find anyone who would claim me."

"Most folks don't want to raise someone else's kid."

"Yes, I know. But Dad wanted children, lots of them. Mother didn't. After she left I was all he had. He soon became so attached to me that for years he lived in fear of someone coming to claim me. Later he realized that I'd no more leave him than he would me."

The sun was straight up when LaRoche rode back in to report that the trail was clear.

"There's a plain with good grass up ahead," he said. "You can make it by night if you move them along."

Benson turned to O'Quinn.

"Let's throw them on the trail as soon as possible," he said. "We'll make that plain by nightfall, let them get a belly full of grass and then shove them along. Maybe, just maybe we can make it to Sumner in time to get Raphael to a doctor."

"We'll make it," O'Quinn said. "We'll make it by the hair of a billy goat's chin or bust ourselves trying." He whirled his mount and once again a musical "Yiii! Yiii!" echoed across the plains as weary cattle were prodded onto the trail by equally weary riders.

And another weary rider moved out ahead of the cattle. A rider who slumped in tho saddle and rolled with the rocking pace of a blue mare.

CHAPTER 14

An ancient cottonwood, struggling against the years, and against dry seasons that had become more pronounced over the past century, climbed straight up from the rim of a rocky wash in the shadow of the Sacramento Ranges. Seated cross-legged against the bole of the great tree, Chief Ten Bears regarded his braves as they slipped down into the wash and formed a half circle about their aging leader.

One by one they came. Tall Feather in full battle regalia. And Tenawa, who limped heavily from an old wound where a soldier bullet had torn away part of his right knee. Buffalo Kills, Prairie Wolf, Eagle's Wing, and Standing Bear. Each took his place in respectful silence, that their chief might speak first. When all had gathered, they numbered less than a hundred. Less than a hundred of the once powerful Yamparika Comanche Tribe which had, for countless generations, controlled much of the Texas panhandle and those prairies that stretched north up through The Nations. A proud people, who had given way slowly but surely before the white invasion.

Twice, Ten Bears removed the long stemmed pipe from his mouth, and soft curls of smoke drifted in the morning air. And each time his eyes, masked behind an expessionless leathery face, lifted to the shadowy blue mountains that climbed into the sky to the west. At last he spoke.

"Ahead are the Sacramentos." He lifted an arm and gestured with the stem of the pipe. Then he turned in the other direction. "Behind us is our beloved prairie. The land that the Maker of All Things gave to our people from the beginning of time. Today we must decide where to point our moccasins. What say you, Tenawa, the aged? Or you, Tall Feather, the one who is still filled with the fire of youth? Who shall speak on these things?"

Tall Feather stood up, straight, proud. His hand rested on the muzzle of a captured army rifle. His eyes were clear, unafraid. "If we go to the mountains the white man will follow us there. Our people are rested and ready to travel again. Yet must we always travel away from the land that is rightfully ours. Our wounded braves are healed and ready for battle. As the white man measures his intrusion into our land in miles, so do we measure our losses in numbers of warriors and squaws and children."

He paused while his eyes swept the semi-circle of warriors about him. "Those who wish may go to the mountains," he continued. "As for me I would die in the land of our fathers."

A murmur of approval ran the full length of the half circle as Tall Feather sat down. Then Tenawa stood up, favoring his game leg. He carried many more years than Tall Feather, more even than Chief Ten Bears. His hair was white, his face cut deep with heavy lines.

"Only five moons have come and gone since our chief journeyed to Medicine Lodge Creek." Tenewa addressed himself to the braves about him. "There Chief Ten Bears met with men from the great white father in Washington. They wish us to go onto a reservation, like cattle in a pen. There the blue dressed soldiers will oversee us. The same soldiers who came with the Utes to burn our lodges and kill our women and children."

The eyes of the aged warrior swept the half circle and returned to the chief. Eyes that did not see as clearly as they once had, but eyes that were still filled with fire.

"Each of you know one thing," he continued. "They do not speak with straight tongues. They have never done the things they promised. I would join Tall Feather. I am old in the ways of our fathers. My days are now few. Those days that remain, I would spend in the lands of our fathers. If I must die to stay there, then die I will."

Ten Bears pulled heavy on the pipe.

"You speak well, my braves," he said. "It was not we who first drew the bow against our white brothers. It was not my warriors who first killed women and children. Yet when they did these things to us we took the road behind them. We made them cry. If my warriors will follow me we will

80

make them cry again."

As one, the warriors stood.

"We only await the word of our chief," Tenawa said.

Ten Bears rose slowly. He knocked fire from the long stemmed pipe and rubbed it out with a moccasined foot.

"Standing Bear and Eagle's Wing have scouted far," he said. "They bring word of a wagon train that is many sleeps from Fort Sumner. The wagons number more than three times the fingers on both hands. And they travel without soldiers."

The chief paused while a murmur ran around the half circle.

"Two sleeps will take us beyond the Pecos," he said. "Three more will place us on the trail before the wagons. We will take from them food to replace the buffalo they took from us. We will take clothes to replace the buffalo robes our women and children no longer have."

"It is good," Tenawa said. "Our spears are ready. Our quivers are filled with new arrows. We have many soldier rifles. That we go back to our beloved prairies is very good."

Tall Feather had been the first warrior to arrive. When the meeting was over he was the first to leave. He sprang up the steep bluff and crossed to where the women were skinning game. His medicine had been very good this morning. In the early hours he had killed a pair of antelopes with the soldier rifle. He had lashed their legs together and packed them in on his horse.

"Fix me the liver," he said to the tall woman who stood up on his approach.

"This thing I will do," Tanda replied.

Tall Feather turned away. He began to climb a nearby mesa. Chief Ten Bears, coming out of the wash, watched him. He marvelled at the lithe, powerful body that was goaded on by the fire of youth.

"If I had five hundred warriors like him," he said to himself, "I would take on the whole of the white man's army."

On the following morning, while the stars still looked down from the heavens, and before the morning bird first voiced a song, Tall Feather led his saddled mount before a white buffalo hide tepee. He lifted the door flap. Tanda stepped forward in the light of the lodge fire.

"We go now," he said simply.

"May the Maker of All Things go with you," Tanda replied.

They did not touch, did not kiss. There was no goodby, no tears. For a long moment they looked into each others eyes. In that moment Tall Feather was seeing again the beauty and grace that had led him to ask for the hand of Tanda in marriage. Dark hair, with the sheen of the raven's wing fell in a great mass about her shoulders, framing a face that had once laughed with him.

Now they did not laugh. They had not laughed since the soldiers, with the help of the Utes, had killed their young son in that raid back on the Canadian. Yet there was love in those dusky eyes that looked deep into the soul of her brave. And he knew he would take that love with him wherever his moccasins pointed.

Quickly the warrior dropped the door flap. He stepped into the rawhide saddle and rode into the night. His mount's unshod hooves beat a rhythmic tatoo with the others about him. He did not look back. He knew that he might never again lift the door flap to that tepee. Yet such was the way of the Comanche, the way of life that had been thrust violently upon them. A way of life they had no choice but to accept.

It was a grim band of warriors that moved out that morning. There had been no war dance, no war paint. Those things had gone out with the old ways. Life now, even bare existence, had become deadly cold business for the Comanche.

Ten braves were left to guard the camp and provide meat. All others joined the raiding party. They hit a steady, relaxed gait. They were horsemen, as good as the prairie had ever bred. They knew how to pace their mounts -- how to get the most out of them.

They swung a little south of east, pointing their course to the Pecos. They would cut deep enough into the south to avoid a clash with the white man's Cavalry stationed at Fort Sumner.

Ten Bears had dispersed his warriors. He had seen the Cavalry travel by squads. So had he spread his men. Scouts were out on the point, the flanks. There was little chance of a confrontation here in these barren wastes. Yet caution was what had kept the Yamparika Comanche from complete annihilation.

Tall Feather was on point. Ten Bears wanted him there. The deer bladder canteen that Tanda had filled the night before hung from his belt. A rawhide bag, tied to his saddle, bulged with ammunition, as did a similar bag of jerky. He, like the others with whom he rode, had prepared for a long journey. The soldier rifle lay across the pommel of his saddle. He rode out from under the stars, and into the rising sun. He held a steady gait and did not pause for a break until his shadow told him it was high noon.

CHAPTER 15

For two days the herd coursed north without event. North by the steep banked Pecos that grew smaller, yet swifter as they climbed up through The Territory. North with all the speed the riders could muster. They threw the longhorns on the trail before daylight and drove into the night. Weary riders sang and talked to themselves to keep from falling asleep while riding nighthawk.

The condition of Jan Raphael's leg grew worse each day. Benson and Lore rode up one flank and down the other, urging the riders to greater effort.

One group of twenty-odd trail weary steers broke away. Three of them were dead by an alkali waterhole before Weaver and Hagerman could round them up. Other groups broke away, mostly of smaller numbers Some were left behind because of the urgent need to push on to Fort Sumner.

About noon of the third day LaRoche came loping back in, his mount at a dead run. Lore and Benson, riding off the right flank, saw him first, then O'Quinn and Weaver.

When the old scout came in sight, he lifted an arm and circled it, indicating to turn the herd.

O'Quinn spurred his horse forward and began to press the point. Weaver, working the far side, dropped back and let the line bend. Lore rode forward to put pressure on the flank, and Donnel, riding farther back, loped up to add his support. The others joined them. It was all methodical. Weeks on the trail had built the riders into a team that worked together like a fine tuned piece of machinery. Within minutes the longhorns were swinging into the inevitable circle that would bring the moving mass to a grinding halt.

Benson rode out to meet LaRoche. The old scout slid his blue mare to a stop. For the first time Benson saw a change in the man's leathery expression. Whatever was out there on the trail had his complete attention.

For a long moment LaRoche sat with his eyes glued to the cattle, making certain that they were turned, that they went no farther up the trail. When the point was headed back toward the river he breathed a sigh of relief. Then he came about and his weary eyes fixed on Benson.

"Comanches," he said. "Most I've ever seen in one party in all my years of scouting. They're coming out of their stronghold across the river, moving east. And we don't want to stop them."

He paused briefly while his eyes turned to his own back trail.

"Pass the word," he continued. "No shooting. No noise. No fires. Move the cattle in against the river. Hold them there in cover."

Without waiting for further information, Benson touched reins to the stud's neck. Partner spun around, lunging out as he felt his rider's weight shift forward in the saddle. Within ten seconds he was hitting top speed.

Benson paused briefly to talk to Lore while LaRoche alerted Donnel and moved on down the east flank. Benson moved on to pass the word to O'Quinn, then around the point and down the river side. Now, as in previous moments of tenseness, he found a strange feeling of strength in the powerful animal that flowed along beneath him, bending quickly to his every cue.

When he finally arrived back at the wagon, Benson found LaRoche asleep at the base of a giant cottonwood. Apparently the old scout had regained his composure. He sat with his back to the tree, his hands folded on his lap, his head dropped forward on his chest. He had loosened the saddle cinch and slipped the bridle so the mare could graze while he slept.

The wagon flaps were open, and Benson rode over to see Jan Raphael. The man's thin lips seemed to grow whiter each day, and his hands trembled. But fire still glowed in the deep brown eyes that looked out of the great hollows that had formed around them.

Benson took a swing around the herd, making certain that the cattle were being contained. When he returned, he found LaRoche up and ready to go. With nothing more than a gentle nod of his head, the scout mounted and pulled his mare about.

They loped their horses north for about a mile, then pulled down to a walk to avoid making a dust trail. The sun beat down on their backs and they welcomed the cool, damp air that came up from the river.

LaRoche turned right across a bold hump that climbed up from the valley floor to form a long irregular mesa. Abruptly the scout drew up and dismounted. He signalled Benson to do likewise. They led their horses into a clump of cottonwoods and tied them off.

LaRoche struck up a small ravine that climbed to the crest of the mesa. Cover was sparse, but the old scout climbed with the stealth of a stalking cougar. They held to the left face of the ravine, so that anyone riding up from the river would be less likely to see their trail.

The higher they climbed, the closer LaRoche clung to the ravine trail. By the time they reached the crest of the mesa, they were bellying along like a pair of oversized lizards.

From their new vantage point, they could survey the plains that swept out to the northeast, shimmering in the heat, and fading to blue haze in the distance.

LaRoche took a small telescope from a worn leather case on his belt. He pulled out the sections, and focused on the plains stretching away to the north. He rested the scope on a clump of earth and lay very still.

Without a glass, Benson could see dust trails that crawled like tiny threads into the east. It wasn't a large army of braves. Rather it was scattered little groups, riding like dispersed cavalry squads.

"What do you make of it?" he asked, after the old scout had watched the caravan for many minutes.

"Maybe a war party," LaRoche said as he passed the glass to Benson. "But I don't think so. Looks more like a buffalo hunt."

"There aren't many buffalo left to hunt," Benson said. "But there's cattle. Lots of herds trailing up through The Nations to the railroads in Kansas."

"I'd lay you a wager they know what they're after," LaRoche said. "And if I was guessing I'd say there's a wagon train out there on the prairie. And if I guesed again, I'd say it includes a sizeable number of wagons to get that much attention."

Benson studied the riders, but the glass told him little more than what he already knew -- that they were Comanche braves, travelling east.

"What else do you read from it?" he asked.

"Do you see the packs?"

"I hadn't noticed, but now I think I do. Nothing big, but I see what you are talking about. Does it mean anything?"

"Indians travel light," LaRoche said. "They live off of the land. When they do carry essentials it means they're on a long journey, usually several days. If I read it well, and we stay out of their way until they all pass, we might cross their land without trouble."

"I hope you read it well," Benson said as he lowered the glass and passed it back to the scout. "We need a break. If we don't get one, Jan will never make it."

LaRoche was a patient man. It took a patient man to scout this wild land, and to stay alive in this untamed wilderness. And he had stayed alive through more than a quarter century of scouting the plains. For an hour after the dust trails disappeared in the east he continued to watch the prairie below them. Then another hour. Benson's patience grew short. Still, the old scout lingered.

The sun had dropped behind the mountains to the west before LaRoche stood up. He folded the glass and put it away.

"Best to be sure," he said. "If there were more to follow they would have passed by now. If we move fast enough, there's a good chance we can get through before the warriors get back."

In the cottonwoods they found their horses and mounted up. They walked until they reached the river, then sent their mounts south at a fast lope. Swinging around the big bend of the river, they slowed to a walk when

87

they reached the cove where the herd was gathered. Already the cattle had been bedded down, and the soft song of the nighthawks drifted on the twilight breeze.

Lore had heard the pounding of hooves, and rode out to meet them.

"What did you find out?" she asked.

"We saw a large party of Comanche warriors moving east," Benson said. "LaRoche here thinks they'll be gone for several days. If he's right, we may be able to get through their land without any trouble."

"Then you bring good news," Lore said. "I sure can use it. Dad's running a fever and his leg is turning dark."

"Then he's worse," Benson said.

"Much worse."

"That's too bad." He turned to LaRoche. "We've been knocked off schedule again. How far do you think we are out of Sumner?"

LaRoche dropped his eyes, fingered his chin.

"Four hard days at the most," he said

"Then we'll make it in three." Benson wheeled the stud and sent him across to where O'Quinn and Weaver had dismounted and were letting their horses pick at the bunch grass.

"They've had a good rest and are full." Benson said, looking out over the herd. "We'll head out an hour before daylight tomorrow, and keep them moving until night stops us. If we don't keep pushing, Jan Raphael might not make it."

Weaver looked up at Benson, his black face darker still in the shadow of night. His brow knotted.

"Mister Raphael is worse?" he asked.

"Much worse," Benson said. "Even if we push our hardest, Lore isn't sure he can make it."

"Then we'll push even harder!" Weaver flipped the reins over his mount's neck.

"If it's for the Boss," O'Quinn said. "We'll bust our guts trying."

He swung into the saddle and turned to Weaver.

"Let's line out the riders tonight so there'll be no confusion in the morning darkness," he said.

Kirk Weaver nodded, stepping into the saddle. They rode off toward the herd.

Benson rode back to the rear of the wagon where Skip was stacking wood and setting the cook pots. Together they staked out a couple pieces of canvas as a shield to help contain the light from the fire. Then Skip set the blaze and started coffee brewing. Grumbling to himself, he began preparing the evening meal.

One by one, the riders ambled in and filled their cups. They dropped down in the light of the fire, sitting in groups of twos and threes. Raphael called from the wagon, his voice sounding weak and far away. Lore climbed into the wagon, then came back to send Skip in to help the wounded man.

Somewhere from out across the plains the wavering call of a coyote sounded. LaRoche stood up. He cupped a bony hand to his ear and tilted his head at an angle.

"Sounds real," he said. Still he stood his rifle against a wagon wheel and stepped off into the shadow.

Others stood up, listened, then dropped back, secure in the knowledge that the old scout was out there looking to their safety.

Lore trailed the red roan out into the night and mounted. Benson followed and together they rode off toward the river.

The stars were coming out, one by one, frail hesitant lights twinkling in the great blue dome that swept up from the mountains. They rode in silence, listening to the night sounds, and the gentle grating of iron horseshoes in the sand.

A burrowing owl screamed in boisterous protest, then drifted away on soundless wings. Back on the plains the coyote wailed again, a mournful call in the new night.

"I hope it's real," Benson said.

They pulled up on the river bank.

"We talked this evening about Skip cutting off Dad's leg," Lore said. "Skip would have to cauterize the stump with a hot iron. Dad wanted to wait until we reach Fort Sumner. Surely they have an army doctor there."

"I feel certain they do," Benson said. "All army posts have doctors."

"We may be in time," Lore said. "But I don't think so. Dad will never go back down this trail, Benson -- neither will you."

"I'll go back," he said. "Maybe not now, but I will."

"You were right that night when you said it sounded as though I would be sorry to get to Fort Sumner."

She threw back her head to the heavens. Almost unconsciously, she lifted her hair and let it fall about her shoulders. Even the pale starlight cast a sheen on the velvety strands that fell about her face.

"Yes, Benson," Lore said, "you were very right."

He pulled the stud in close and reached across to grip her hand.

"I've got a job to finish," he said. "And when it's over, I'll be free to go where I want and do the things I want to do. I'll find you, Lore. I swear I will. Wherever you are, I'll find you."

"Yes," she said with bitterness, "unless there is another job, and then another. And somewhere out there is a bullet with the name of Nathan Benson scrawled all over it. That's the way it happens out here -- the way of the west."

"You don't understand," he said. "I'm not on a hired job. I've never killed for money. I didn't want to bother you with my problems when you have so many of your own. But now I want you to know."

He paused, waiting for her reaction. He realized that he had never told anyone his full story. And just now it seemed to have lost some of the importance that he had attached to it before.

"I guess it all started a long time ago," he said. "I was one of those hot-headed Texans who rode off to fight for a cause we thought was just. Maybe we were right, maybe we were wrong. It doesn't matter now."

He was feeling his way, watching her. Talking about himself was something new to Benson.

"I was twenty one and ready to sprout wings and fly away," he continued. "It just seemed the most natural thing to go to war. In my mind it was a fanciful, thing--riding through captured towns, waving to the grateful people we had just liberated. But it turned out to be different. It was hell, Lore. Just like Sherman said.

"After Appomattox, I headed home. You don't feel real good down inside when you are beat -- not when you have pride. I was feeling pretty low. But I wanted to get back home to Texas, back to Mom and Dad. On the way, I traded my last food for this fellow here." He leaned forward and patted the neck of the black stud.

"He was just a spindly little colt then, a short three year old. He was ewe-necked and half starved. But there was fire in his eyes and strength in his slender legs.

"From that first moment we had faith in each other -- this stud and me. We started the long journey out of Virginia, angling down through North Carolina and across the deep south. When there wasn't food for two I saw that he ate. We were on the road for two months, working when there was work, but mostly just living off the land. And he did get me back to Texas. But there was no home, anymore. No Mom, no Dad."

He felt a lump in his throat and he looked away at the mountains that stood pale blue in the night.

"While I was away, my father was shot down in the streets of Waco by a man I'd never heard of, named Shack Cumby. Mom, they told me, died of a broken heart. I couldn't even find her grave. When I got to our ranch, I found out that it had been taken over by Bandy Parker and his son. I was met by a sawed-off shotgun in the hands of Bandy's son. He hustled me off my own land. That's about all there is to the story."

"Not quite," Lore said. "I think it's still going on."

"The stud and me, we hit the trail. There was nothing else for me. For two years we've scoured the southwest, looking for Dad's killer. If it takes two more years we'll keep riding. It's something I have to do."

"I understand how you feel," Lore said. "Vengeance is something we all look for at one time or another. But it's a dangerous thing. Right now I'd like to ride back to the hills and hunt down the man who shot Dad. Hunt him down like I would a coyote. But I won't. I wouldn't, even if I knew who and where he was."

"You wouldn't have to," Benson said. "I'd go after him myself. So would a dozen other men."

They sat in silence for a moment, listening to the babbling of the river, the frogs that thrumped and peeped from its banks. Then they heard the shot. Only one.

"That came from the camp!" Lore said.

"Yes. And it wasn't LaRoche's .50 caliber." They wheeled their mounts and rode out through the darkness.

O'Quinn stood by the fire. He looked up when Benson and Lore loped in out of the night. His expression was one of amused irritation.

"Scoop thought he saw something out there in the dark," he said, anticipating their question. "Must have been some animal. We looked, but we didn't find any tracks."

Benson touched reins to the stud's neck and sent him around the fire and across to where Hailey stood apart from the other riders.

"You trying to stampede the cattle?" he asked. And his voice was sharp with reproach. "Or maybe you're trying to get the Comanche's attention?"

"Thought I saw something move," Hailey said. "Looked big enough to be a man."

"Suppose it had been?" Benson said. "LaRoche is out there! Suppose it had been him coming back in and you'd shot him?"

"Okay," Hailey snapped. "Suppose it had been?"

His face was ashen. His beady eyes glinted in the firelight. There was challenge in his expression.

"I'd have put a bullet between your eyes," Benson said. "You keep that gun in your holster where it belongs, or I'll take it away from you."

Benson turned and rode back toward the fire. From the corner of his eye he saw Buttons a little apart from the other riders -- his hand on his gun butt and his eyes on Scoop Hailey.

Lore went to the wagon to check on her father. LaRoche drifted in out of the night like the fleeting shadow of a cloud.

"Heard a shot," he said. "Trouble?"

"Hailey got trigger happy," Benson said. "Thought he saw something in the darkness and took a shot at it."

LaRoche looked across at the wrangler. Something like a low growl formed in his ancient old throat.

"Bad medicine," he said and turned his attention to the cook pots.

CHAPTER 16

Away to the north, yet closer now as the giant pincers of the plot pulled together, Shack Cumby circled his wagons and drew them tight in against the night.

Lance Kimball made his final swing about the camp. When that was done, he rode back into the camp circle, uncinched his saddle, and wiped down his horse. Cumby sat on a cottonwood log pulled up by the cook fire. Kimball dropped his saddle beside the log. Then he walked to the fire and poured himself a steaming cup of coffee.

Cumby looked up at Kimball.

"Still wish you were back in Texas?" Kimball asked, not looking up from his pouring. "You still got a place there?"

Kimball took a seat beside Cumby on the log.

"Nope," Cumby said. "Wasn't much of a ranch anyway. That was down Lorena way. I guess I could have made it into a fair spread with some work. But I spent most of my time looking for my daughter, Morning Bird. Never could seem to get my mind on ranching."

"Morning Bird?" Kimball seemed puzzled. "Hadn't heard you speak of her before. Or maybe I shouldn't ask."

"It's alright," Cumby's voice grew heavy with emotion. "She was only five when I lost her. Her mother had died the year before, so I took Morning Bird with me wherever I went. One day, I was looking for some steers that seem to have dissappeared. We got bushwacked by rustlers. I hid Morning Bird in a sage thicket and tried to fight them off. They hit me and left me for dead. I didn't come around for two days, maybe three. I wasn't sure. I couldn't find the child, so I figured the rustlers had taken her.

"In the years that followed I covered every rustler cove in Texas and a few in the Territory. I ran down a hundred bad leads. Each time, I died a new death at the end of each empty trail. I know she's out there somewhere.

I know also that someday I'll find her -- unless Benson finds me first."

"Reckon she'd be about growed up by now."

"I've seen fifteen summers come and go since I lost her. She was a pretty kid. She'd be about twenty now. Freckles across her nose and hair the color of a raven's wing. Glistened like velvet when the sun was full on it."

"Come and get it!" Shank bellowed.

Cumby took a tin plate and cup from his saddle roll and filled them in silence. He returned to the cottonwood log.

Countless stars wheeled overhead and an owl twittered somewhere out on the plains. Kimball returned with his plate, then dropped to the log and shoveled down his food like a famished wolf.

"You ever run into Nathan Benson?" The scout polished his plate with sand and stood up to return it to his saddle roll.

"I came close once," Cumby stared into the fire. "Only once, in a saloon in Sherman. I was in a poker game with three other gents when I heard someone asking about me at the bar. The bartender, who didn't know me from Adam, told him he'd seen me heading west on the Butterfield Trail. I guess he thought it would earn him a fat tip. That's when Benson started west. And me, I turned back the other way. Headed for Missouri. Then I took this wagon train so I could get clear out of civilization. And that's where I am."

Cumby put away his plate and cup and the two men crossed the circle of light. Abruptly Cumby paused and turned to the scout. Firelight glinted across his face accentuating the anxiety written there.

"Lance," he said. "Have you ever heard of Kandee?"

"Who hasn't," Kimball replied. "I ain't just heard of him, I seen him. In a gunfight down Loredo way. Saw him shoot two gringos for beating up an old man."

"He's fast, they tell me."

"Faster'n all hell. Them gringos drew first, both at the same time. Kandee

95

shot the two of them between the eyes before either got off a round. And he only had one gun."

"You know who Kandee really is?"

"Never heard him called anything else."

Even in the darkness Cumby's eyes bored into those of the scout.

"Lance, Kandee is a handle he picked up in the army. His real name is Nathan Benson."

"Whooeee!" Kimball whistled between his teeth. "Sure wouldn't want him on my trail."

CHAPTER 17

The next day, LaRoche and the blue mare had long since paced out into the shadow ahead of the herd, scouting trail for the day. When morning broke, he would be perched on high ground, where he could watch the plains for miles around. Then he would move again, farther up the trail. It seemed that he never grew weary of that monumental task -- looking to the security of others. So maybe, just maybe, with the Comanche threat almost passed, and with only outlaws to deal with, this first herd might make it up through The Territory to Fort Sumner.

Call them rustlers, outlaws or whatever. But they were the one great menace that had plagued the drive throughout the long weary miles. Were they out there again? O'Quinn knew of one herd they had taken. And if they had succeeded before, there was no reason to expect that they had gone away.

Benson rode point with Nardi O'Quinn. For days now, that red-bearded giant had rode with his left arm splinted and strapped in to his body. He had performed as completely as any other rider. And always there had been a broad grin that even his red beard could not hide. But today Benson noted something strange about the man.

O'Quinn was silent. He answered questions briefly. He appeared nervous. His eyes flashed up and down the trail ahead, as if he were looking for something, expecting something

At intervals Benson dropped back to circle the herd, keeping the riders pulled in close and well spaced--keeping the steers moving--getting every possible mile out of that long wavering line of longhorns. At mid-morning he swung back by the wagon, where Lore was staying close to Jan Raphael.

"How's he taking the ride?" he asked.

"Not good at all." Her voice was grave. "He's out of his head most of the time. When he is conscious, he's in severe pain. The jarring of the wagon is almost unbearable. Could you help me pack the blankets in closer around him?"

Skip pulled up the team while they climbed into the wagon. Working together, they lifted first one side and then the other, moving more padding in to help absorb the sway of the wagon. Raphael opened his eyes once and looked up at them.

"Thanks," he said weakly.

Skip whipped up the team and the wagon rolled on. Again the black stud swept up one flank, and down the other.

"Keep them moving!" Benson shouted. "Keep them moving!"

One by one the riders took up the cry.

"Keep them moving!"

Spurs touched wiry, high strung cow horses. Sullen steers bellowed. Sweating riders shouted, cursed, leaned from their saddles to lash at stragglers.

"Keep them moving!"

And the mass of long horned critters flowed across the hard, dry earth like a turbulent stream.

They kept the herd moving until night closed in on the Pecos. The banks of the river had grown steeper, making watering difficult. O'Quinn volunteered to scout ahead and look for bedgrounds where there was grass as well as access to the river.

The steers were turned and gathered in against the river bank. And once again the mournful wail of nighthawks floated out across the prairie.

While the first shift of riders calmed and bedded the cattle, the other riders drifted in out of the night on saddle weary legs. They dropped in a ragged circle about the fire Skip had kindled. Some sipped at their scalding coffee. Others, too weary even to talk, just stared at the flickering flames.

Like a part of the night itself, weary old LaRoche came quietly into the circle of light. He slipped the saddle and bridle from his mare and came to stand by Benson.

"No fresh sign," he said. "Another hour and we'd been pretty well out of

Comanche land. They'd take us on easy on their own range, but they keep their distance from Sumner and the cavalry."

"We'll make that hour before day comes again," Benson said. "And what about outlaws?"

"No sign," the old scout's brow knotted, and he asked, "Where'd you send Hailey?"

"Hailey?" Benson looked puzzled. He turned to survey the trailhands around the fire.

"I didn't send him anywhere," he said. "I thought he was here."

"I met him about a mile north. Heard him coming and thought he might be a Comanche scout, so I hid by the trail. He didn't see me."

"What do you figure he was up to?" Benson asked.

LaRoche's dark eyes flashed in the firelight.

"He wasn't just going for a ride in the night," he said. "He was on the gray Arabian and he was sure'n hell hauling the freight to somewhere!"

O'Quinn, who had been listening from where he slumped on the ground, stood up.

"That gray's the fastest horse in the remuda," he said.

The three men walked out to the remuda, their tired feet dragging in the sand. Hailey's mount was there. His sweaty, dust-caked coat showed that his rider had not taken time to groom him. And the gray was gone.

"He cut out," Benson said. "Guess we're better off."

"I wonder if anything else is missing?, O'Quinn said.

"He couldn't have taken any supplies without Skip seeing him," Benson said.

They were walking back to the wagon when O'Quinn paused abruptly and turned to LaRoche. His face was serious, his brows drawn as he looked at the scout.

"Did you see a bold mesa out ahead, on the right side of the Pecos?" he said. "Crowds close down to the river. So close that the trail between it and the river is real narrow."

LaRoche stroked his chin with long, bony fingers.

"About four, maybe five miles up the stream," he said. "Came through there this evening. It's steep, and pretty well covered with shrubs."

"That's the place." O'Quinn snapped his fingers. He turned his face out to the night with eyes narrowed as though he was reliving a vivid moment.

"That's where we were hit last time."

He turned to Benson.

"That's where we were hit the last time," he said again. "And I'm beginning to remember something else -- something that I don't like -- don't like it a bit."

"About the other drive?" Benson asked.

"Yes. The other drive. Now I'm wondering about this one too. You remember I told you Hailey was with us then. Well, on the night before the outlaws ambushed us, he rode out. Said he was going to try for a deer at daybreak, that he was tired of beef."

"Did he get his deer?"

"No. He said he saw a nice doe but she winded him and ran away before he could get a shot. It sounded good then, especially when he wasn't the only one tired of beef. We'd run out of rations the week before. So I had no reason to question him then. Now I'm remembering other things. Like just how the rustlers knew the exact time we would be driving through that pass."

"When did he come back?"

"Just about daybreak the next morning. Couldn't have had much time to hunt and get in when he did. I swallowed the story then, all of it. Now I'm beginning to wonder."

"Do you think it's possible that this might be a repeat performance? That maybe he's out there somewhere making a contact tonight?"

"Sounds kinda far fetched," O'Quinn said. "Maybe I'm letting my imagination run wild. But I've had a strange feeling all day. Like an omen of something bad that was about to happen, I'm not one to spend my time worrying, but there's something about this situation that has me bothered."

"You said once before that he was the only rider not hit by a rustler bullet. Do you think that was just a coincidence?"

"Just seemed like one of those things at the time."

"Could he have had an opportunity or the time to contact the outlaws after the fight?"

"Could have. I thought I was the only one to escape until he caught me three days down the trail. He was so much help to me while I was packing that bullet, it never occurred to me to question him."

"Did he seem to have a roll of money, like maybe he'd got a payoff?" Benson asked.

"Scoop never flashes money. But I've never seen him broke."

They moved back to the wagon. LaRoche brought his mount in and saddled her.

"Be back at daybreak," he said.

"Good luck," Benson called.

"Good luck to you if I don't have good luck," The old scout's face showed a rare trace of a smile. "If I don't get back by morning, move out. Cross the Pecos about a mile up. Try for a run north on the other side."

With a flip of the reins LaRoche was gone. The blackness of night swallowed him up. And the sound of steel shod hooves, grating in the sand, died away.

Lore turned to Benson.

"I hope he makes it," she said.

"He'll be back," Benson said. Yet his eyes held to the dark void where LaRoche had vanished.

"He'll be back," he said again.

CHAPTER 18

From afar they watched and waited. A waning moon climbed out of the east while they talked. The fires in the circle of wagons burned low, the voices from the wagons stilled. Somewhere out on the prairie, a wolf wailed long and loud. Then the silence of the night took over. In that silence, Ten Bears and his warriors made their plans.

"You have scouted well, my warrior," Chief Ten Bears spoke to Tall Feather, the young brave standing before him. "You have led us to their encampment."

"That is so, my Chief," Tall Feather replied. "Yet it is your wisdom that we will need in battle tomorrow. From where I watched today I saw many men, many rifles."

"We have left no tracks before them," Ten Bears said. "We will drop far back, let the wagons string out. Their scout will go ahead. Surprise will be ours. The things we are willing to fight for will be ours."

"Tenawa, you will take twelve warriors to the south and wait," Ten Bears said. "When the wagons move out, you will hear the call of an owl, repeated twice over. Then you will attack. Do not ride too close. Fire a few shots, loose a few arrows, then ride out again."

"This thing I will do," Tenawa said. "so they will run."

"You speak well, old one," Ten Bears answered. "When they run I will signal Tall Feather. He and his warriors will come down from the north. You will come back then, to cut off the wagons before they can circle."

"It is true that they made our women and children cry," Tall Feathers said. "But then we did the same to them. Must we do this thing again?"

"We will not hurt the women and children," Ten Bears replied. "We want only the things we need. These things we will fight to get."

Tenawa began to select his men. Tall Feather stepped out into the night. A dog barked from within the circle of wagons as the wolf wailed again. And the men of the plains drifted back like silent shadows in the wan moonlight.

Lance Kimball heard the wolf's cry from where he sat on the cottonwood log. It was real. He was certain of that. Yet that strange sixth sense that the outdoorsman develops unconsciously and cannot explain, was goading him into action. The hackles on the back of his neck seemed to be trying to lift up his hat. A strange tingling sensation climbed up and down his spine: He stood and turned, listening to the night. His ears strained for a sound, but none came to him. The prairie night was deathly silent after the wolf's cry. The dog barked once more, then retreated beneath a wagon and was silent.

The wind was out of the west. No plains Indian would come in with the wind.

He expected trouble from one or more of the Comanche tribes to the south. But as certain as the moon rose up out of the east, so would that trouble circle and come in from another direction. He had watched the back trail well that day and held it in little fear. This left only the north.

That was why Shack Cumby's scout slipped out from the circled wagons and headed north. The urge within him was great. So great that he ran the first quarter mile before he dropped back to a fast walk. Then slower, his moccasined feet padding silently on the dry prairie ground. After another quarter mile, unexplained sounds came to his ears. He bellied down and began to crawl. That was when he heard the shuffle of unshod hooves. Thirteen he counted. Thirteen mounted warriors, riding single file, riding east.

He lay glued to the ground where he had taken cover behind a clump of sage until the riders were long gone. He was about to stand up when he heard a horse blow somewhere out in the distance. Again he crawled forward until he came to the encampment: He saw no warriors but there were horses, many of them. And their number told him that a large party of Comanches were just waiting for daylight. He turned and began to crawl away.

The sky in the east lightened. Dawn filtered out across the prairie. A new day, gray in its beginning, yet destined to turn blood red on this tiny niche of the great plains.

Chief Ten Bears watched the wagon encampment, his bronze face masking the emotions throbbing within him. There were signs that he did not like. Horses that had been hobbled out beyond the circle of wagons were gone. They had been brought inside during the night. Riding horses were already saddled. The teams were harnessed but none were hitched. Instead all were tied on the inside of the wagons. Morning fires had been beaten out. Women and children had retreated into the canvas covered wagons.

A buckskin clad rider came out to circle close in about the wagons. A big man on a big horse rode beside him. Still no teams were hitched. No effort had been made to break camp.

Men with rifles slipped about within the circle. They lowered boxes from the wagons and removed wagon seats, using them to block the spaces between the wagons, building a breastwork. Behind this they dropped with rifles protruding over the top. Others crawled beneath wagons and thrust their guns through the spokes of the wheels.

The Comanche chief knew now that something had gone wrong. What, he didn't know. They had come in with the night. His braves were well concealed. They had left no tracks before the wagons. What he could not know was that the uncanny plainsman he had seen circle the wagons was three-quarters Chickasaw. Nor could he know that he had been schooled both as a Chickasaw wolf and as a cavalry scout.

Tall Feather fretted inwardly. When the morning was half gone he left his cover and began to crawl through the sagebrush. He reached a point where he could see the encampment and lay with his eyes glued to the wagons. He wished now that he had gone in last night as he had wanted. But Chief Ten Bears had insisted that no tracks be left about the caravan. That would take away from the surprise he had hoped for. A surprise that now had been lost.

The sun burned down on his back and his young muscles ached for action. Yet he lay as immobile as a stone until he saw Chief Ten Bears stand up, off to the south. Quickly Tall Feather rose above the bushes. He heard the sharp spang of a rifle but he was out of range. He heard two more reports, both of which kicked up dust well before him.

Instead of the call of an owl, to signal an attack, Tall Feather heard three sharp coyote yaps. This was the message to gather. He dropped back to where the horses were hidden, mounted and rode around to the south with his braves following.

"We will join Tenawa," the chief said when they had gathered. That and nothing more. He began to make a wide circle, out of rifle range.

Tall Feather let his braves pass, following the chief in single file. They were walking their horses, saving them for the violent action that would come later.

When all of the warriors had passed, Tall Feather fell in at the rear. Those braves out before him were a splendid lot. Courageous men who dared do battle against terrible odds rather than submit to bondage. Their feathered lances, held high, streamed in the wind. Their bronze legs gripped fast the sides of their lean, hard ponies. These men of the plains rode tall and proud.

Tenawa had held his men in cover on the back side of a low mesa. He rode out now, and the small army of Comanches lined up on the crest of the mesa.

Chief Ten Bears took his place at the center of the line. Tall Feather and Tenawa rode in to confer with him, then dropped back to either end of the array.

These moments of waiting for a signal to attack were tense moments for Tall Feather. He had ridden this line before, when it was five times the length of this one today. And one by one he had seen his fellow braves go down. One by one, and sometimes, by twos and threes. A few who had been wounded had recovered. But most had died on the field of battle, and the hard earth had swallowed them up in as many unmarked graves.

He saw Chief Ten Bears lift his long feathered lance. The war whoop of the Comanche rose again. The war whoop that had sounded back on the banks of the Canadian and the Arkansas -- that had rung out in bitter retreat from the homelands. It was not so strong now, yet every brave took it up. And, as one, their ponies lunged out and began to press down the slope.

For an instant Tall Feather thought of Tanda. An image of her passed before him. The slender dark eyed maiden who had been filled with laughter when they played together as children. That had been deep in the heartland of what the white man now called Texas. Only an instant. Then he was riding low on his pony, swaying from side to side, firing as he rode.

They came close enough for those with bows to loose a flight of arrows. Then they swung out and circled the caravan.

From one of the wagons, someone screamed in pain. A man stood up behind a wagon, clutched at his breast and went over backwards. Then a horse squealed, breaking loose and lunging between the wagons to lope out across the plain, tug chains jingling behind. Puffs of black smoke arose from the makeshift breastwork. The war whoop of the Comanches blended with the roaring rifles, a single chorus rolling across the plains.

They completed the circle and Ten Bears led them back onto the mesa again.

"We will wait," he said. "Rest our horses. Let them worry."

Rifles still sounded from the wagons, but their bullets fell short of the line of warriors. Soon even they stopped, and all was quiet.

Ten Bears called Tall Feather in to confer. He signalled Swift Eagle to join them, for Tenawa was no longer there. The aged one lay motionless on the prairie down below. He had returned to the land of his fathers, the land he loved. And he had died where he wanted to die.

Two other braves had gone down. One lay still. The other, Sleeps-In-The-Wind, showed signs of life. When they made the next sweep someone would be designated to pick him up.

Buffalo Kills had been hit in the left shoulder. Still he sat straight on his mount, unmindful of the trickle of red that came down his side and spread out over his buckskin breeches.

The riderless horses had followed the warriors back to the mesa. Tall Feather and Running Antelope dismounted and picketed them to bushes.

Ten Bears now gave directions for the next attack. Tall Feathers was to swing left, take the lead. Swift Eagle would fall back to the far right and bring up the rear. When they moved out he wanted them to scatter, stretching the line to three times its present length. Then they would swing like a great half moon, riding across the south side of the circled wagons. Twice they would ride by, just out of rifle range. This would draw fire from the frightened defenders. Then, on Ten Bear's signal, they would swoop in and out, in and out. Three times they would harass the wagons. Then they would call for a truce. They would barter peace for the supplies they needed.

No need to hurry now. It might be two moons before another wagon train rolled this way. And cavalry patrols would not extend this far from Sumner unless they were alerted.

"What if they could get a messenger through to Fort Sumner?" Tall Feather mused. The thought struck him like a blow from a spear shaft.

"Maybe we should circle the camp," Swift Eagle said, "to keep anyone from escaping."

Tall Feather determined to ride back at once and confer with Ten Bears. But even as he pulled up on the mouth rope of his mount, he saw the lone rider.

Lance Kimball had rode his leggy pinto out between the wagons on the northwest bend. In a flash he was loping across the prairie, trying for an end run. He knew the Comanche party could hack the train to bits, hour by hour if they determined to do so. The only chance of survival for the caravan lay in the Cavalry stationed at Fort Sumner. If they were to be alerted it would be up to him to do it. He could not know that the Comanches had barter in their mind, and that there was another way out.

Tall Feather wheeled his pony and gave chase. A barrage of gunfire from the circled wagons attempted to turn him, but the bullets kicked up dust well short of where he rode. And even if they had not been short he would have ridden on.

The Indian pony was smaller than the pinto, but he was carrying less weight. He was accustomed to pursuit and his muscles were as hard as spring steel. And when his rider leaned forward and shouted in his ear, he lengthened his stride.

Tall Feather swung wide, avoiding the rifle fire. For a time it seemed that the scout would get away. But the young warrior had no such intentions. He knew his mount, knew his staying power. And he knew how to ride with the animal moving beneath him -- an animal that could run for two miles without slowing his pace. When he cut back on the scouts trail, he called again on his mount. And the little pony dropped closer to the ground. The gap between the pursued and the pursuer began to narrow.

Lance Kimball glanced over his shoulder. He saw what was happening.

He was losing the race. His leggy pinto did not have the power that the pony behind him had. He drew his heavy .44 Remington service revolver, a gun he had retained from his cavalry scouting days. He fired two quick shots over his shoulder and lashed at his mount's flank with the reins.

Tall Feather heard the bullets whiz by. He leaned lower and brought his rifle up. He was close now, close enough that he would not waste his cartridges. He lined the rifle and squeezed off a shot.

He heard the dull thud of lead striking flesh and saw the shock that flashed through the scout's body. But the bullet had not been good. He knew that from the way the man sat the saddle, the way he rode. He lifted the rifle again and heard the hammer fall on an empty chamber.

Dropping the rifle he clawed at the throwing axe lashed to his belt. His pony's nose was within a dozen feet of the pinto's rump. Only a scant minute and he would overtake the man. He drew the axe.

Only seconds now. He raised the throwing axe just as Lance Kimball whirled in the saddle. The scout fired point blank into Tall Feather's chest.

The heavy .44 ball struck him like a rock thrown from a cliff. It drove him back out of the saddle. He lost his axe as he clawed to keep from going off. He pulled himself back into the saddle. He felt faint. Still, if he could only catch this man, he would kill him with his bare hands.

The horse and rider out ahead of him began to blur, then spin. Soon the whole earth seemed to be whirling around. Tall Feather pulled up on the mouth rope. He knew now that he had lost the chase. A mind picture of Tanda flashed before him and he knew also that he would never again lift the door flap to the white buffalo hide lodge off there in that arid land where his people had been driven.

The obedient pony stopped. Tall Feather sat slumped, his head on his chest. And slowly, ever so slowly he slid from his mount and lay quietly on the dry earth that already was drinking up his life's blood.

CHAPTER 19

In the gray of early morning Lore rode out to where Benson sat upon Partner, watching the herd, watching the trail north. There were hard lines about his eyes.

"You've heard that the stars can tell us what's in store for us?" Benson asked, a faint smile crossing his face.

"Yes." Her eyes held his.

"Well," he said and he wasn't smiling now. "If you could read our stars, I'm afraid you'd see a rough day ahead."

"I'm sure you're right," Lore said. "Did Hailey come back?"

"Slipped in last night."

"Have you talked to him?" Lore asked.

"No. I want to talk with LaRoche first."

"Do you think he knows you're suspicious?"

"He's jumpy. But I don't think he knows we're onto him. O'Quinn isn't letting him out of sight."

"We should be moving out," Lore said.

"We'll be on the trail shortly. But I won't let the wagon go out until LaRoche gets back."

Soon, the sound of running hooves came in out of the morning shadow. La Roche pulled to a sliding stop and dismounted. He walked directly to Benson's black stud and looked up into the eyes of the man who was ramrodding the drive.

La Roche's ancient eyes, narrowed now, were still bright, filled with the fire of life. He hesitated. He was not a man given to emotion, yet there was a note of excitement in his manner.

"O'Quinn was right," he said. "Completely right. That one over there, he met the rustlers somewhere up the trail last night."

He gestured at Hailey, who had just slipped out from behind the remuda and was watching them.

"Then he brought them back to the pass O'Quinn talked about. That's where they are now. About twenty, maybe more. I couldn't be sure in the dark. They're in good positions. If we moved in unawares, they'd empty half our saddles before we knew what hit us."

Hailey played with the remuda ropes, his beady eyes glued to LaRoche and Benson. Benson motioned to O'Quinn to come over, and explained the situation.

"What's our best bet?" O'Quinn asked.

"We could cross the river," LaRoche said. "Going's rough over there, but we could try a run up the other side."

"If we did they'd likely move on up and cut us off again," O'Quinn said.

"Right now, we know where they are," said Benson. "Later we may not."

"That could make all the difference," LaRoche said.

Benson looked out to the north where the shouts of irritable cowmen and the bellow of protesting cattle mingled in a common sound.

"We have to deal with them," Benson said slowly, his jaw set, his eyes cold and determined. "Just as well get it over with now."

"And Hailey?" O'Quinn questioned. "What do you plan to do about him?"

"I'll talk with him," Benson said. "Give him a chance. If he won't talk I'll prod him into going for his gun."

"I've asked Buttons to drop back and pick up the remuda," O'Quinn said. "I had the feeling that Hailey wouldn't be travelling any farther with us."

All the while they were talking, Hailey stood by the remuda, watching them. Even though he was too far away to hear them, the wrangler was suspicious. The old scout had been out all night and, he acted as if he had brought news of interest.

A wave of cold fear flowed through Hailey's body. He had overplayed his hand, and now they were on to him. With the two gunmen's backs turned, he saw his chance.

In one motion the wrangler dropped the remuda ropes and whirled. His feet were planted hard where they struck ground, his body tensed and he leaned slightly forward. And his gun hand had already flashed down to his holster and was coming back up.

Lore had not dismounted as the others had. She was the first to see Hailey move.

"Benson!" she screamed.

Lore clawed at her own gun and lunged the roan forward in an effort to place herself between Benson and the wrangler. But even as she drove her spurs into the roan's flanks, she knew she would be too late. Already the man's gun was out, swinging into line with Benson's heart.

Benson lunged away, whirling and drawing. O'Quinn leaped in the other direction. Both men had drawn their guns by the time Hailey had his bead on Benson.

The sharp crash of a .36 Navy Colt revolver ripped the air. Hailey dropped his gun. His left hand clutched at his breast where a dark blotch was flowing across his shirt.

With dogged determination, Scoop Hailey fought to stay erect. His head went back, his mouth opened and the color went out of his face. He went down with a thud and lay still.

Benson looked at O'Quinn, then at Lore. They stared back at Benson in puzzlement. Neither had fired.

Then Benson saw Buttons, off to the left. The man's dark eyes were still fixed on Hailey. His .36 Colt, the muzzle tilted slightly up, trailed a thread of black smoke.

When Buttons was satisfied that Hailey would not be going for his gun again, he dropped the .36 Colt back into his holster. He looked at Benson and lifted his hand to his hat. Then he stepped up into his saddle and rode over to the remuda.

Benson holstered his .44. He gathered Partner's reins and swung into his saddle.

"Don't that beat all," O'Quinn said.

"We got careless," Benson said.

Benson turned to LaRoche. "Can you get yourself and two men into a good firing position on the mesa above the pass?"

"Two men or half a dozen," the old scout said. "You give me the men. I'll put them where they can make themselves known."

"We can't spare that many from the drive. Maybe we could give you three. With your gun that would make four."

"I'll go," O'Quinn said.

"I'll need you here," Benson said. "I want you to handle the herd."

"Well, hornswoggle me!" O'Quinn said. "You're going to run them through the pass!"

"But that's what they want!" Lore said.

"I don't think so," Benson said. "Not the way we're doing it. Send Donnel, Dailey and Wellman with La Roche. I want to ride out with LaRoche and have a look ahead."

"Leaves me pretty short on riders," O'Quinn said.

"When I find where to start the stampede, I'll drop back and help push them through the pass. Buttons can help with the drag, even if he has to abandon the remuda."

"Oh, we'll make it." The hard blue eyes flared. "By the horns of the holy cow, we'll make it."

LaRoche climbed into his saddle. He gazed off to the north.

"I'll need at least an hour to get the men on top and get them settled in place," he said. "We'll have to swing wide and come in from the back side of the mesa to keep from being seen."

"We'll allow for that," Benson said.

"Leave that to me," O'Quinn said. "I'll set a pace to cover you. When the cattle get them out in the open, give'em hell. And don't forget to throw in a round for Mister Raphael."

"What about Hagerman?" Benson asked. "He doesn't have a gun. I guess he doesn't even own one."

"No," O'Quinn said. He looked out to where Hailey's horse still stood ground tied. "I'll get Hailey's rifle for him. He doesn't need it anymore."

"Lore," Benson said. "Have Skip keep the wagon up close until we run them. Then he can drop back until the pass is clear."

Benson hesitated.

"I'd rather you rode with the wagon," he said.

"Thank you for your concern, Mister Benson," she said. "But with Dad dying in that wagon from a rustler bullet, I don't have much patience with cattle thieves. If there's any fighting going on, I plan on being a part of it."

Benson caught the fire in those dark eyes framed with strands of velvety black hair. And for a moment he looked deep into that fire.

"I know how you feel," he said gravely. "Maybe that helps you understand me."

Benson wheeled the stud.

"Let's move'em out!" he yelled.

"Git dogies, git!" The drive swung out. A thousand sets of cloven hooves pounded the hard earth, grinding it into dust. Trailhands hazed in the stragglers, urging them back into the long line. Still, they came. Two, maybe three hundred laggards feeding sullenly into the drag.

When the drive was on the trail and the cattle had settled down to a steady plod, Benson rode forward with LaRoche and his men. When they reached the point where LaRoche would leave the river, they paused.

"There's a bend you will have to make to get the cattle pointed through the pass," LaRoche said. "Get close enough to see that bend. But don't forget that the lead gunmen are close in against the butt of that hill at the pass."

With that the old scout turned right and hastened his men around to the back of the slope.

Keeping well concealed in the cover LaRoche had suggested, Benson crawled forward until he could see the entrance to the pass. At the narrowest point, the corridor was little more than a hundred yards wide. And going into the pass, the trail made a gentle bend to the right.

If he could send a rider in to lead the point steers, they would probably make that turn without crowding any into the river. But he knew that would be too risky. Riding ahead of a stampeding herd on good ground was dangerous. He would not risk a rider on a trail that might have unknown obstacles on it. They would just have to start into the bend, and hope for the best.

The slope above the pass was lightly covered in scattered timber. Heavy clumps of low brush grew along the river bank and in against the base of the hill. Possibly migrating herds of buffalo had kept the center of the corridor free of timber.

Benson noted that the trees here climbed much higher than those farther south. He reasoned that the area must have more rain. That prompted his attention to the clouds that swirled over the mountains. Even as he looked up, the clouds moved in, blotting out the sun.

Working his way back, Benson made mental pictures of the landmarks where he would start the run. Then he went back to where he had hid his stud Partner in a clump of low growth cottonwoods.

CHAPTER 20

When Benson loped around a bend and came in sight of the herd, he pulled up suddenly. It wasn't altogether the sight of Hagerman riding point that shocked him. Quiet, reserved Dexter Hagerman, who up until today had refused to carry a gun.

What really threw Benson was the rider's dress. For when Hagerman had picked up Hailey's rifle, he also took the wrangler's vest and hat. And he was riding the gray Arabian, the mount Hailey had ridden when he met the outlaws.

"A get-up like that is likely to get you killed," Benson smiled as he pulled the stud around and fell in beside Hagerman.

"Maybe by you," Hagerman said. "But not by the men up there. I'm riding point through the pass. And I'm counting on this outfit to keep lead from coming my way."

"It's too dangerous," Benson said. He took a long look at this mild mannered man who had suddenly determined to ride at the head of a stampeding herd of Texas cattle.

"You've spent fifteen years herding longhorns for Jan Raphael," Benson said. "You know what can happen to you, out in front of a herd of frightened steers."

"I know the risk," Hagerman said. "I've seen it first hand. But I'm leading the cattle through the pass."

"You could swing up on the face of the hill after you get them started through," Benson said. "That would get them on the way, and put you in a good shooting position to boot. You and Weaver are the only J-Bar-L riders on the drive. I'm sure Jan and Lore will be counting on you and Weaver to get them back to Texas, especially with Jan knocked out the way he is."

"Lore," Hagerman said. " Yes, Lore. Unless you're taking her back. Jan won't be going back to Texas. He died this morning."

Hagerman turned to look at Benson and his soft brown eyes were suddenly hard.

"I talked with O'Quinn," he continued. "He's going back to Texas. He'll help Lore out if I don't make it."

"You'll do more good alive than trampled to bits by that herd back there."

"If I stay out front, those longhorns will follow me. I want them in that pass, Benson," There was bitterness in his soft voice. "And I want me a rustler. One for Jan Raphael."

"If you must do it," Benson said. "Forget the rifle. Leave it in the saddle boot. Keep your eye on the trail. Ride low and ride like hell."

"This gray will get me through," Hagerman said. "What's the starting signal?"

"Two shots close together."

"See you on the other side," Hagerman said, as Benson spun the stud and sent him back along the flank of the drive.

"Guess Hagerman gave you the bad news," O'Quinn said as Benson pulled up.

"How's Lore taking it?"

"She's hurting bad, Benson. Hurt, mad as hell, and brave all at the same time. She's bringing up the drag. I tried to get her to ride with Skip on the wagon but she wanted to keep busy. And we really need her."

"You're keeping them up tight for the small crew you have," Benson said. "Did you put Weaver on the river flank?"

"He's an old hand with longhorns. I figured if we had a man that wouldn't let them push him into the river, it was Weaver." O'Quinn's eyes were the hard blue of deep and turbulent pools. And there was no laughter in them now, only cold and calculating death. "Weaver will be ready. In fact, we're all ready, Benson. Ready to run these crazy critters and ready for one hell of a fight."

"When we get them going," Benson said. "I want you and Weaver to pull back from the flanks. Give them room to spread out. I want that corridor full of cattle, from the river bank in tight against the butt of the mesa. And I want them moving at full speed. We'll lose a few head on the trail, a few in the river. But I think they're going to do the job."

"I hope you're right," O'Quinn said, his eyes sweeping first the cattle, then the trail ahead.

"I hope so too," Benson said.

"You riding back to see Lore?"

"Yes, for a few minutes. Then I'll be back to give the starting signal and help getting them in action. We'll run them in about a quarter hour."

Benson wheeled the stud, riding along the irregular flank that came and went like the bellows of an accordian.

Lore rode out to meet Benson. He swung his mount around and fell in beside her. She wasn't ready to talk yet. He could see that.

Benson pulled in close and reached across to grip her hand and found it clinging to his.

A steer bellowed in sullen protest, then another and another. They had grown accustomed to long hours and hard drives, but they still didn't like it. They were on the prod, ready to run at the drop of a leaf -- burning with a lust to unlimber their trailhardened muscles, muscles that had carried them this far across the earth in a seemingly effortless gait. Dust lifted from the trail, ground to powder by a thousand sets of cloven hooves, a thousand and then a few more. A dense yellow cloud drifted away to the east on a brisk wind, boiling and tumbling as it went.

"I'm sorry," Benson said at last. "Sorry for you Lore, and sorry that Jan didn't live to see the drive through."

'Thank you," she said. "I'm sorry too. Sorry, not just for Dad, but for the other men we've lost. And we'll lose more men in that pass up ahead."

"I'm afraid it's too late to think about that."

"We could try crossing the river. Maybe make an end run around them."

"If I tried to do that I'd have two fights on my hands," Benson said. "Those rustlers out there want this herd. And they'll have them unless we fight for them. They'd come after us in a minute if they knew we'd stopped or turned. But first I'd have to fight Jan Raphael's men. You're hurt, Lore, but they're hurting, too. Hurt and mad and spoiling for blood. If I didn't detest thieves so violently, I think I'd almost feel sorry for those men in that pass up there. They're going to catch hell before this morning is over."

"I know you're right," Lore said. "But I hate to lose more lives. It just all seems so terrible to me right now."

Benson looked across at the sea of needle pointed horns that lifted and floated, like wavelets before a storm about to break.

"If I'm not wrong," he said, "those longhorns over there are going to clear the pass without much loss to the drive. Maybe a few head of cattle. Maybe a rider or two. Maybe none."

"I hope you're right," Lore said. "How far are we from the pass?"

"We're almost there," he said, jerking erect as though he had momentarily forgotten time. "Be careful, Lore. I must hurry."

He loosened his reins and pounded up past the long wavering line of sullen steers.

Riding wide, Benson waited until Hagerman was within sight of the point where the trail bent back through the pass. He wheeled Partner in toward the flank. As if in warning of what was to come, a dozen raindrops pelted him.

A steer rolled his eyes and hit a fast trot as Benson rode in. He drew his gun and fired two rapid shots. Black smoke spurted out across the herd. As if the heavens were acting in concert with the drama playing out below, thunder rolled across the sky and fingers of lightning darted toward the earth.

The steer lowered his head and lunged out. A bellow of fright came up out of his throat as he crashed away. Other shots sounded. Riders shouted and beat at the edgy animals, giving them the excuse they wanted. Fright flowed over the herd like a wave on the ocean.

Soon a thousand head of lunging cattle were in full flight. Now, Hagerman let out the Arabian as the lead steers pounded along behind him. They swung into the pass with the inevitability of a fast freight on steel rails.

"Push 'em!" Benson shouted. "Move 'em on!"

But his voice was lost in the rumble of steamroller motion that gushed along the trail. He pulled Partner away and sent him toward the slope above the pass. Leaping low bushes and boulders, the faithful animal carried his rider to a command position on the steep butt of the mesa.

From this position Benson could see the entire trail through the pass. Farther into the pass the trail, which had appeared clear at its throat, was strewn with boulders, buffeted with trees. They would lose some cattle in there, for certain. And Hagerman's only chance of survival lay in the nimble legs of the Arabian that now swept him along before that sea of sharp hooves and deadly horns.

Weaver and O'Quinn dropped back from the flanks, and the cattle spread out, choking the corridor from the river bank to the base of the mesa. They were running at full speed now, heads lowered, with a synchronized rhythm, as unstoppable as a flash flood roiling through the pass.

Four rustlers, hidden in a thicket up front to seal the pass after the drive moved through, saw what was coming. Too late they came out of their cover. They yelled as they raced for a clump of greasewood where their mounts were tied, throwing their rifles aside in their haste. But it wasn't enough. Their horses had already broken free and bolted ahead of the cattle.

Benson had his rifle out and to his shoulder, but there was no need to use it. A steer dropped his head. A longhorn ripped through flesh and bone.

The outlaw was thrown into the air like a wisp of paper. The wave swept over the rest. Sharp hooves ground them into the earth. And the stampede rolled on.

In the wild melee, riders and rustlers alike were scarcely aware of the lightning that played over the Pecos. Nor could they hear, over the thunder of hooves, the thunder rolling out across the plains like a cannonade. But no one missed the rain that poured suddenly out of the sky -- a violent shower descending in great sheets.

In the blinding rain, two rustlers, hidden along the river bank, made it to their mounts. Lashing madly at their horses' flanks, they raced along the open trail out ahead of Hagerman and the cattle.

Benson rode out the face of the mesa, trying to keep pace with the herd. As soon as it had begun, the rain ended, and Benson saw the fleeing rustlers. He lifted his rifle just as the stud leaped a fallen log, tripped and went to his knees. With enormous brute strength the animal surged back up and lunged on out the slope.

By now Hagerman had his rifle up and going. He had dropped his reins and was firing point blank at the outlaws. In his urgent desire for vengeance he seemed to have forgotten the wave of death that flowed swiftly, violently along the trail behind him.

"Hagerman!" Benson yelled "Ride!" But his words were lost in the din and rush of the stampede.

Hagerman was firing wildly, squeezing off shots as rapidly as he could lever in a fresh shell. His lack of experience was showing now. He became more frantic with each miss.

At last a wild bullet caught the lead horse in the neck and sent him down. Too late to swerve, the second horse fell over the first and both riders were sent spinning in the trail. Both came up and both lunged for the one good horse that got to his feet and plunged away in fright. One caught the saddle horn and swung up. The other was left afoot in the path of the oncoming cattle.

Benson's gun was up now. Two quick shots and the horse raced away with an empty saddle. He was turning back to the man on foot when he saw the Arabian falter. He shouted wildly but his words were ground up in the confusion almost as they left his lips.

As he had fired, Hagerman had thrust the stirrups forward. The Arabian, a trained cow horse, misread his actions and set his feet in a sliding stop. Too late the man saw his error. He raked the gray's flanks with sharp rowled spurs.

Benson lifted his rifle and dropped a steer behind the Arabian. Then another and another. But it did no good. They came on like an ocean wave at high tide. Mad now with fright, the cattle leaped and lunged, oblivious to what lay before them.

A steer lowered his head. A long horn ripped open the belly of the horse. A horn from the other side swept up the horse's back and drove Hagerman from the saddle. Horse and rider went down under a sea of pounding hooves, and Benson turned away.

The cattle came on, frantic now. A few head were pushed into the river. Some were pushed onto the butt of the mesa and were slowed by heavy brush. Others stumbled on boulders and fallen logs and went down to stay. The wave swept over them as a log rolls over pebbles.

Frightened rustlers came out of hiding farther up, routed like quail before a scythe. Those who made it to their horses raced ahead to spread the word.

"Stampede!" came the cry. "Stampede!"

It rang through the pass. Men clawed at leather, lashed their mounts wildly. Those farther up heard the cry and knew what it meant. The trail riders were forgotten. No time now for them. The cattle the rustlers had come to take were taking them.

A .50 caliber roared down from the crest of the mesa. It was followed by a barrage as the lever action rifles opened up. Bitter men fired with deadly purpose. Bitter men who looked for vengeance and found it below them. Saddles were emptied, still they fired.

Five outlaws managed to get beyond the range of those rifles.

Another rustler came up the river bank. He heard the firing, saw the puffs of smoke from the crest above him. He swung into the thickets along the bank and somehow got through the hail of lead.

Six outlaws raced off to the north. Only six of the twenty odd men who had waited in ambush. Waited to kill and to steal. And the cattle they had waited to steal now came through the pass and swept along behind them like a monster of death.

LaRoche watched the escaping rustlers through his glass until they melted into cover at the bend of the river. He folded the glass away and hurried to his mount. He booted the heavy rifle, stepped into the saddle and sent the blue mare lunging down the butt of the mesa. He was out in the valley before the drag had passed. He let the mare blow while the stragglers lumbered by. Then he crossed the trail, swung in by the river and loped north. As the stampeding cattle slowed, he raced along the left flank.

When the old scout had passed the longhorns, he picked up the trail of the six outlaws. Like a hound in the wake of fresh spoor, he held to the prints of the steel shod hooves. Mile after mile he followed, urging his mount to her utmost. When at last the pursued slowed their pace, he emptied an outlaw saddle with a single shot from the big Sharps rifle.

As the five remaining men scattered and raced away, LaRoche gave up and turned back to where the trail riders were gathering the cattle. And, had he known that Jan Raphael was dead, he would not have quit the chase.

CHAPTER 21

On the banks of a small feeder creek, the cattle were gathered together and built into a trail herd again. What stragglers that could be readily rounded up were fed back into the drive. Those few that had wandered far were left behind. They crossed the stream and swung out northwest. Nardi O'Quinn was on point and Donnel and Weaver were up front on the flanks. Old LaRoche and his faithful blue mare were out front, setting the course to Fort Sumner.

With the herd in motion again, Benson rode back to the wagon where Lore and Skip Bonner waited to pull out. He reined in, stepped from the saddle and took off his hat.

"You want to bury him on the trail?" He gestured toward the wagon. "We could put him in a grave over there next to Hagerman. Maybe it wouldn't be as though he were all alone."

Lore looked out toward the drive that now trailed slowly to the north.

"No," she said firmly. "Not here. He said he would drive to Fort Sumner come hell or high water. They both came and he won't know it, but he'll be with the herd when it reaches the end of the trail."

Lore nodded to Skip. He moved the wagon slowly down into the water, crossed and climbed the far bank, rolling in the wake of the herd. Lore and Benson rode behind the wagon.

After they were away from the mesa the going was less rough for the wagon. Skip whipped up the team. He caught the drive and held close to the drag. Benson and Lore rode out to prod the drivers to extra effort, and to remind them that there would be no grazing time and no cook fires kindled until they were in sight of Fort Sumner.

So once again the cry of the Texans sounded from the rim of the herd. "Git dogies, git! Git along that dusty trail to Fort Sumner--fast!" And the longhorns, wearied from the morning run, were content to settle into that long trail-eating stride that marked the endurance of the beasts from time immemorial.

It was late evening when a whoop went up from Nardi O'Quinn. It was picked up by the flank guards and passed along. The trailriders whistled, shouted, and laughed.

"Fort Sumner!" O'Quinn cried.

The word was magic, filled with excitement. It was the climax to a long and ardous struggle -- a victory cry.

Lore and Benson let out their mounts and loped forward to look upon the first evidence of civilization they had seen in many weeks now. And a pleasant sight it was. The old scout had already made contact. He was now returning, bringing with him a detachment of cavalry to give the riders from Texas an official escort.

O'Quinn left the point and rode out to join Benson and Lore. There was now laughter in those hard blue eyes, that only this morning, had been filled with the desire for vengeance.

No need to hurry now. They were here. The three slowly rode forward to meet the men from Fort Sumner, savoring the moment. This was the moment they had hoped for, had prayed for. And now that it was here it seemed almost unreal, like the ending of a fairy tale.

Captain Sam Scott introduced himself as he loped up with LaRoche in advance of the detachment. He rode erect, with that certain dignity that enhanced the image of the frontier Cavalry. He gave a snappy salute as he greeted the trio. He surveyed the long line of steers -- watching them crawl across the brown earth like a multi-legged monster.

"Your scout here tells me you drove them critters all the way up from Texas," he said.

He addressed himself to the riders, but his eyes still held to the stream of longhorns. They seemed to fascinate him.

"Yes," Benson said. "Through Apache land, Comanche land and rustler land."

"Did you have any problems with the Comanches?" The military man's blue eyes narrowed as they swept the woman with the raven hair, then came to rest on Benson.

"Guess we were lucky there," Benson said. "Or maybe just fortunate to have an excellent scout." He gestured toward LaRoche. "Had a scare with the Mescalero Apaches, but they wound up bailing us out of a mess."

Captain Scott shook his head. "Those poor devils on the Mescalero Reservation are hungry," he said. "We need to do better by them."

The military man turned once again to the cattle.

"This is what we're needing," he said. "we haven't been getting beef in sufficient quantity to feed them."

"You've got beef now," Benson said. Then he added, "If the price is right."

"How many in the drive?" Scott asked.

"Little over a thousand," Benson said. "We started with better than fifteen hundred."

"I don't know what you expect to get out of them," Scott's eyes narrowed as he studied the Texans. "We'll pay twenty-two dollars a head and take them all."

He watched the look that passed from Benson to Lore and on to O"Quinn.

"That's the fixed price," he hastened as though in second thought. "The best the Army will pay. Can't go a dollar higher."

Lore nodded consent.

"We'll take it," Benson said.

"Throw them off the trail and hold them until morning," Scott said. "Well pay you for them tomorrow and take them off your hands."

Captain Scott watched the weary riders drifting by. Abruptly he turned back to his detachment.

"Sergeant Huskins," he called.

126

A three-striper, dressed in full regalia, left the troop and loped forward, looking almost as heavy as the little mustang he rode.

"Send Corporal Dirk back to the fort to round up a dozen drovers and get these men some help. They look like they are about ready to drop."

Sergeant Huskins saluted and rode away.

"These rustlers you had trouble with," Scott said. "I hope they weren't on this end."

"Both ends and the middle," Benson said. "We got hit south of the Territory. Then again, in the middle where the Apaches came to our rescue. The last ones were just south of here, less than a day's drive. Seems they wanted us to do all the driving for them before they took over. But we fixed them up real good."

"How many were there?"

"About twenty two, best we could count of what was left of them," Benson said. "We think only five escaped."

"Sounds like you've done most of our work for us," Scott said. "If your scout can give directions to Sergeant Huskins, we'll send out a troop and round up the five who got away."

"LaRoche will help you with that," Benson said. "In fact, the way we feel about rustlers right now, we'll be more than happy to help any way we can to run them down."

"We have some good troopers," Scott said, "I assure you, we'll run them to earth and bring them to justice."

"Now we have another problem I'm sure you can help us with," Benson said. Briefly he told Captain Scott of Jan Raphael's dream of opening up a trail and his brave but futile battle with his shattered leg. "We'd like your help with arrangements for a funeral."

"I'll send out an ambulance wagon for him right away," Scott said. "The man deserves recognition and the least we can do is give him a decent burial. I'll set the services for ten o'clock tomorrow morning, if that suits you?"

"That will be good," Lore said.

"We can finish the business transaction after the services," Scott said.

Lore and Benson thanked Captain Scott and turned back toward the wagon. Nardi O'Quinn loped out to turn the herd that was slowly feeding north.

"Fort Sumner," Lore said. "Dad planned and prayed over this drive until it just had to happen. And I believe the Lord sent you to help him, Benson. I don't see how we could ever have made it without you."

The ambulance wagon, drawn by a pair of white horses, arrived at dusk to carry away the body of Jan Raphael. With it came Captain Sam Scott and an honor guard, for the man who had conceived the first successful drive up from Texas was a hero to the people of this remote outpost. Soon, more-Texas longhorns would be driven north. And the National Trail, even then a hotly debated issue in far away Washington, D.C., was soon to follow the hoofprints of this Texas herd --out of Texas, then up through the Territory, through the land of the Apache and the land of the Comanche. And from there, on to Raton Pass into Colorado. So, though Jan Raphael could not know it, he was to be received with honor at Fort Sumner.

Benson and Lore mounted to ride in with the ambulance.

"You take over," Benson said to O'Quinn, "After we see to the arrangements for Jan, Captain Scott has invited us to dine with him in the officer's mess. Lorena's going to eat with her feet under a table once again. Then I'll see if the Captain can put her up in the officer's quarters, at least for the night."

"A real sit-down meal sounds wonderful," Lore said. "But I'm not staying in the officer's quarters. I'll spend the night out here, under the stars, with the herd and our riders, just as I have all along."

CHAPTER 22

The funeral was a simple service, held in the little chapel in back of post headquarters. Captain Scott placed a flag at the head of the casket and furnished an honor guard. The sermon was given by the post chaplain, who eulogized this man from Texas who had successfully organized the cattle drive, then given his life that a trail might be opened up through the Territory.

On a little knoll in back of the chapel, a grave had been opened in the dry, hard earth. Lore sobbed softly on Benson's arm as the bugler sounded taps and a rifle squad fired three volleys out over the grave.

Lore, Benson and O'Quinn had lunch with Captain Scott. In the afternoon, additional drovers were sent out from the fort to help the trail riders count the steers.

Eleven hundred and twenty two of the fifteen hundred head had completed the drive. Captain Scott was elated. He beat Benson on the back and squeezed Lore's hand.

"We've tried every way we knew to get beef in over the Santa Fe Trail," Captain Scott said. "But we haven't been able to. We've decimated the buffalo herds that these Indians survived on. Now we have an obligation to them."

"There are plenty more cattle where these came from," Lore said.

They rode back to post headquarters. Captain Scott calculated the price and counted out a fourth of the amount due Lore. He slid it across the table and gave her a draft for the balance, with payment to be made at Fort Stockton in Texas.

"You can use my office to pay your men," he told Lore. "Then I hope you will be staying at the post for a spell before you start back to Texas. Your men look like they could use some rest."

"Only a couple of days," Lore said. "I have to get back to the ranch. Things will be different now, with Dad gone. I know that. But I must go back and face up to it."

"Too bad it had to happen this way," Scott said. "But you can never really know what Jan Raphael and the rest of you have done for this country. Cattlemen have been dreaming of this trail for years. Now, you have made the dream a reality."

"Yes," Lore said, "but at a terrible price."

Scott started for the door then turned.

"You can use my office as long as you like," he said. "I have arranged quarters for you, Mr. Benson, and the rest of your men in our quarters. You're welcome as long as you would like. And when you decide to trail back south, I'll furnish you an escort."

"Some of my riders have agreed to see me back," Lore said. "LaRoche will scout for us."

"That's all fine," Scott said. "But you might be less lucky with the Comanches going back. I'll furnish you an escort, at least until you get through Comanche territory."

"I don't think we'll have any problem with Mescalero Apaches," Lore said.

"We'll have beef to the Apaches, probably before you get there," Scott said. We'll send them out with an escort, possibly in the next couple of days. You may just want to tag along with the drive."

Then he smiled, and added, "Since it's been so long since you were on a drive."

Lore took the seat behind the big unfinished oak desk. Benson sat at the end to help her with the count. One by one, the riders came in and drew their pay. O'Quinn was paid for a trip up and back, as was Bonner, Donnel, and LaRoche. Kirk Weaver, the only J-Bar-L rider left, drew his monthly wage and paused before the desk, his black face pinched and tired.

"You're a mighty pretty paymaster, Miss Lore," he said. "But we do miss the Boss, don't we?"

Benson drew his pay last. Lore counted out the four hundred dollars.

She hesitated a moment. Indecision played on her face.

"Shall I count out for a return trip?" she asked.

"When I go back it won't be for money."

He stood, and helped her gather up the change and stow it in her bag.

"I'll be back at five," he said. "O'Quinn will keep an eye on things until I get back."

"Bonner says there's a wagon train due in right away with lots of goods from back east," Lore said. "I'd like to have a look. Maybe buy something pretty for myself."

"O'Quinn, Donnel and I are all on the same floor here with you. We'll arrange to get you out to the market at any time you wish."

Lore thanked him and closed the door. He wandered down the dark and musty hallway to his own room.

Once inside he locked the door and removed the money belt he wore around his middle. He placed most of his wages in the pockets of the belt and left the rest in his jeans to buy cartridges and other supplies before he rode out on the trail again.

He shaved and bathed and felt like a new man. In his saddle roll he found a change of clothes and dressed. Down the hallway he knocked on O'Quinn's door.

"Let's find a saloon and get something to cut the trail dust out of our throats," he said when the red bearded man came to the door.

"I'll join you on that," O'Quinn said. He took his hat from a staghorn rack beside the door and followed Benson down the stairway. Once outside the quarters, they passed through the gate. A crude board walk led to a small settlement that had already sprung up around the fort. They walked past a blacksmith's shop, a trading post, and came to a rough lumber building with a hand painted sign over the swinging doors that said "Bob Hargrove's Saloon." They went in.

It was dark inside the saloon, and smelled of stale food and sour whiskey.

A half dozen soldiers and cowboys were in the saloon. They lowered their voices when Benson and O'Quinn came in but tried to remain casual. Benson bought a bottle at the bar, and they took a table in the far corner. Following the pattern of western gunmen, they moved their chairs to keep their backs from the bar and the door.

Donnel and Kirk Weaver wandered in. Benson invited them to his table and went back for two more glasses. He popped the cork from the bottle and poured a round of drinks. They had hardly lifted their glasses in a toast, when a trail weary rider dropped rein over the hitching rail out front. He slammed through the batwings and headed for the bar.

The rider's pinched face was lightly bearded. His buckskin garb was covered with dust, and his legs showed the unsteadiness of one who had been long in the saddle. His piercing black eyes swept the room. They caught Benson's, and there was a pause in his stride. Then he turned quickly to the bar.

Benson had the feeling he had been recognized. As his eyes followed the back of the man, he saw the bullet hole in the buckskin shirt, high up on the left shoulder. There was dried blood down his back and a dark red stain oozed from around the hole.

"Whiskey. Straight," the man said.

The barman set up a glass and tilted an amber colored bottle over it.

"Looks like you've been riding hard," he said.

The rider lifted the glass and drained it.

"Hard and long," he said. He rubbed his mouth with the back of his weathered hand.

"Another," he said sliding the glass back across the bar.

Again the bar keeper poured from the amber bottle his eyes fixed on this man of the plains. His dress marked him as a scout.

"Don't reckon you'd be with that wagon train we've been expecting, would you?" the barman asked.

"Reckon I would," he said. He lifted his glass and drained it again. "I'm a scoutin' for them. We've been out from Missouri going on two months now."

"How many wagons?"

"Thirty two when I rode out. Lost three a ways back to Kiowas. Probably a few more today to the Comanches after I left."

"You cut out on them?" the barman asked.

"Hell no!" Kimball straightened. Color flared in the unwhiskered portion of his high cheeks. "I busted through their line and rode in for the Cavalry. The wagons are circled out there, under attack by nearly a hundred Comanches. Some's got lever action rifles and know how to use them."

"How far out are they?"

"Less than a full day."

"Tom Stoddard brought in the last train," the barman said. "He heading this one?"

"Nope." Kimball half turned. He thought he had recognized the man at the table in the corner. He wanted him to hear what he had to say. Wanted to see his reaction to the name. "Wagon master's a man from down Texas way. Name of Cumby. Shack Cumby."

Benson came half out of his chair when he heard the name. His eyes met those of O'Quinn's as he eased back. His lips tightened and his hand gripped the edge of the table.

"Two years," he said. "Two years I beat the bushes and lost every lead I come on. For two years I've always been too late -- sometimes by weeks, sometimes by days. Now he comes to me. Less than a day out on the trail."

"You thought he might have gone west," O'Quinn said.

"Someone told me he was headed west on the Butterfield Trail," Benson said.

"Maybe they were covering for him," O'Quinn said. "He must have gone in the opposite direction to be bringing in a wagon train from the east."

"If I hadn't stumbled onto Jan Raphael's cattle drive," Benson said. " I

133

might be well on the way to California."

"Been best if we'd headed straight back to Texas," O'Quinn said. "Back south with Lore."

"No." Benson's hands played with the whiskey bottle. His eyes stared at its amber contents.

"This has to be," he said. "Best I get it over with."

"Maybe he's fast?"

"He'd have to be fast," Benson said. "He beat Saul Benson. But I still can't believe it was a fair fight."

"You think you can take him?" O'Quinn asked.

"I'm going to," Benson stood up. He tilted the bottle, filling Donnel's and Weaver's glasses.

O'Quinn held up his hand.

"No more," he said as Benson hesitated over his glass. "One a day. That's my limit."

"Let's get out of here!" Benson said, taking his hat and shoving a cork in the bottle.

"Taking the bottle?" O'Quinn asked.

"I'll have another round back in the quarters."

Benson slipped the bottle under his arm and turned to the door with O'Quinn following.

Back in his room, Benson poured a drink. He sat on the edge of the bed, rolling the glass in his hands. He had suddenly come to the end of a long trail. A trail that had seemed like it would go on forever. Now the search was over. The quarry had come to him. And what shocked him was that he found so little enthusiasm for the task that would face him soon, possibly tomorrow. The killing of Shack Cumby.

Somehow the fires of his vengeance had burned low over the past days, or was it weeks? Had they started dying the day he found Lore Raphael back on the Texas plains? Certainly the bitter struggle to get the herd through, the death of Jan Raphael, the hurt he had seen in Lore's eyes, each had taken their toll. But he knew the real reason for his change of heart was his feeling for the woman with the raven hair. It was something beyond his control -- something that seemed to encompass his entire being.

Something inside him had changed. He had, on occasion, played with the thought of giving up his search -- riding back to Texas with this woman who held such promise of fulfillment. The feeling had grown daily, regardless of how much he tried to control it. Now, as he slipped his wages into his money belt and strapped it about his middle, he was dreaming of what that money might buy for Lore and himself.

But he was faced with a shocking reality. He had no choice. He hadn't found Shack Cumby. Shack Cumby had found him. The hunt was over. Only the climax remained -- the duel to the death.

He emptied his glass and stood up. He crossed the room to the single window and drew the curtain to look out on the dreary outpost that was Fort Sumner. Beyond the enclosure he saw the scattered trees, the clumps of buffalo grass, the arid plains that stretched out and away to the southwest. Soft rays of late evening sun came through the window, mellowed now from the burning heat of midday.

Twice he went to the door and placed his hand on the latch before he opened it and went out into the hallway. He was halfway to Lore's room when he paused. He knew full well that it was too late to turn back. There were too many miles in the trail that brought him to this juncture. There was the honor of Saul Benson, the obligation to his father, gunned down in the streets of Waco. He turned slowly and walked back to his room.

Benson sat on the edge of his bed with a third drink in his hands when he heard a knock at the door. He stood up, buckled on his gunbelt and adjusted the gun at his hip. He stepped to the side of the door and opened it with his left hand.

Lore Raphael stood in the hallway. He had never seen her so radiantly beautiful. Her hair, soft and luxurious, hung in dark velvety coils about her shoulders and face. She wore a brown blouse with long sleeves and a high neck, so near the shade of her eyes.

"Come in," he said, hesitation in his voice.

"Thank you, no," she said, her eyes on his. "I just came by to tell you that O'Quinn is escorting me to dinner. Donnel is guarding the bankroll. That leaves you free to take care of your own business."

"I'm sorry," he said.

"We're leaving early tomorrow morning for Texas. If you're not riding out with us, I'll say goodbye now."

"You're not waiting to check out the merchandise on the wagon train?"

"No."

"O'Quinn told you."

"Yes."

"I'll catch you down the trail." Benson was trying to be casual, but he had the feeling that he was making a miserable mess of the situation.

"No," she said with emphasis. "If you're not riding out with me in the morning, don't follow."

"You're asking me to run from Shack Cumby."

"On the contrary, I'm not asking you to do anything. The herd is delivered and sold. You said that ended your contract." She hesitated, then added, "I'd thank you for your services, but I paid you cash for that. All Dad contracted to pay you."

Again she hesitated. There was a slight catch in her voice, and the hard lines about her eyes softened.

"I'll thank someone else for having known you, Benson," she said. "Someone I think sent you our way. I'll never forget you."

Lore turned and walked quietly down the hallway. He heard her footsteps pause and the door to her room close. He turned back to his own room, numb and shocked.

CHAPTER 23

Fort Sumner awoke with the Army. A bugle blared, "You gotta get up, you gotta get up, you gotta get up in the morr--ning." Non-coms barked orders as reveille sounded. A swivel gun boomed as the flag was raised.

Benson had been up long before the bugler. He dressed and headed out to a small eatery he had seen the day before for breakfast. As he entered, a few patrons cast uneasy glances at him. Others whispered to those nearby and nodded. A waiter scurried to guide him to a table, and his overt effort to be helpful irritated Benson. In fact, he had found this particular reaction annoying -- friendly, casual folks who changed suddenly when they learned who he was. Some overdid their effort to be helpful. Others retreated in a frightened manner.

If these people knew who he was, then everyone in Fort Sumner knew. Without question, the wagon train scout had ridden back to tell Shack Cumby. Now, would the man come on into town? Or would he run again? Benson could only guess.

He paid his bill. When he started back to his quarters, the sun was already up. Its rays, mild in the misty morning, held the promise of another hot day.

Benson went to his room to get his saddle roll. On the bed he found a note, scrawled on a piece of brown wrapping paper.

"CUMBY WILL MEET YOU IN FRONT OF THE SALOON AT MID MORNING," it said.

The note wasn't signed and he immediately questioned whether it was a genuine message, or maybe a ruse of some sort. He checked the door lock. It gave no appearance of having been forced. Whoever left the message must have been let in. He determined not to mention it. It may have been an associate of Cumby trying to mislead him. If so he would not give them the satisfaction of knowing he was concerned. Nevertheless, he would be in front of the saloon at mid morning.

At the livery stable he brushed down Partner and saddled him. He filled the magazine of his 1851 Henry and spun the cylinder of the .44, making certain that its six chambers were loaded. He dropped the .44 in his holster. He tied the holster down to his leg with a leather thong and adjusted the belt until the gun hung square over the outer point of his right hip. He drew the gun a couple of times to limber up his wrist Only then did he step into the saddle. He noticed that the stable boy was watching his every move, but he gave him no heed.

There was no one on the street as Benson rode back through town, walking the stud slow. He saw faces peering through windows and cracked doors. If he had been misled, others had too. The town was expecting action. He drew up in front of the saloon and began to wait.

In those tense moments of waiting, Benson's mind wandered, even though his eyes kept vigil. Strange that his thoughts should stray so far from the business at hand. But they did. Back to his childhood days. Back to the wild filly he had spent weeks capturing. There he had known the thrill of success, of possession, but it had all been short lived. She had escaped like a flare of light that same day.

There had been the battle they almost won, but lost. And the ranch he thought was his, but wasn't. Lastly, there was the woman with the velvet hair. With this duel today, he would lose her.

He waited. Waited to strike out and strike down, or be struck down. And always, flashing before his mind, was the woman who had ridden at his side all the way up across the Territory.

Lore Raphael. The thought of losing her left him unnerved, his hands trembling. Quickly, almost violently he pushed her from his mind. His life depended on the speed and accuracy of his gun hand. His eyes swept around, searching for someone to vent his wrath upon, but the street was bare.

It was another quarter hour before he heard the steady clip-clop of a horse. It was coming around the corner with a big man, an old man, plodding slowly toward him.

Benson's eyes fixed on the man. He had expected a dashing gunman in his middle years. He realized there were other horsemen on the street. Three riders came behind the man, all armed.

The big man drew his reins when he was within twenty paces of Benson. He held the reins with his left hand. His right hung loose below his holstered gun.

"Shack Cumby?" Benson said.

"That's me," Cumby said. "And you are Nathan Benson."

"Yes."

"I have no quarrel with you, Benson."

"But I have with you."

Benson's right hand, which rested on the pommel of the saddle, now hung just inches from his gun.

"I came to meet you today, Benson, because I'm tired of running," Cumby's voice sounded weary. "But before there is a fight, I want you to know just what happened in Waco that day."

"Say your piece, Cumby," Benson said. "And make it quick."

Benson heard horses come up the street behind him. He had the immediate feeling that he was surrounded. Shack Cumby had deliberately stalled for time until his men could get in place.

In the blink of an eye, Benson drew his gun and thumbed back the hammer before the four gunmen facing him could get their hands on their guns. Holding his .44 on Cumby's heart, he glanced over his shoulder and saw the big bay with O'Quinn coming up behind him. Along with him were Donnel and Weaver.

O'Quinn stared hard at the men facing Benson. His reins had been knotted and dropped over the saddle horn. His right hand hovered inches above his gun, and the smile that played behind his fiery red beard was the smile of death. Donnel pulled up beside him, his face expressionless, as casual as though he were on his way to the saloon for a drink. Kirk Weaver's dark eyes played over the riders ahead. He rode with his long fingers tensed over the bone handles thrusting up from his holster. They came slowly, pulling up in line with Benson.

"It couldn't have been a fair fight," Benson said.

"You're right," Cumby said, his voice faltering. "It wasn't a fair right. Saul Benson got off two rounds before my gun cleared leather. I was as surprised as he was that those rounds didn't stop me."

Cumby continued, slowly and deliberately, as though he was trying to buy time. But Benson didn't hear him. Instead, he kept hearing over and over again that admission -- "It wasn't a fair fight."

What need was there to talk further. Talk could not bring back Saul Benson. It could not settle an obligation that was even more clear cut now. The man himself had admitted the facts.

"I've heard enough," Benson's voice cut in. "You can go for your gun. Now!"

CHAPTER 24

Lore came down the stairway and out the front door of the quarters. The sun was just coming up as she walked out the stockade gate and down the board walk to the livery stable. The fact that the bag she carried on her arm was heavy with bright new gold coins mattered little to her. She had lost again. She knew she had.

It would be a long trail home. Jan Raphael, the wonderfully kind man she had known and loved as a father, would not be there. Until now, she could not remember ever having been away from him for a full twenty four hours. Not since that day when he had gathered her up on the trail south of Lorena and tossed her onto the bedroll in back of his saddle. And on the heels of that loss, she had lost Nathan Benson, the only man she ever cared for. He had chosen an obligation to kill over the love she had offered him.

Somehow, during their long drive, she had come to believe that she could keep him from killing in bitter vengeance. Last night, she had admitted defeat. He would kill Shack Cumby before the day was half gone.

Lore wanted away. Wanted to get her party together and get on the trail, onto the long road back to Texas.

"Good morning," she greeted the stable boy. "Is my horse ready?"

"Morning, Ma'am," the young man replied. "The red roan?"

His eyes danced with excitement. He must be about fifteen, she thought.

"Yes," she replied. "That's the one."

"Gee, he's pretty," the boy said. "Some day I want a horse just like him -- a good rump, strong back and a deep chest like that. Bet he carries you well and I'm sure he can take a lot of running."

"Yes, he carries well and he can run," Lore said. "He's young, just past five. I broke him myself."

"You with that gunman?" the boy asked excitedly. He saw her start and added in haste, "I mean, Mr. Benson."

"He was the trail boss of the herd I brought in," she said. "We're not riding out together."

"Oh," he sounded disappointed, "He sure packs a peach of a gun. Some day I hope to have a gun just like his."

"Skip Bonner, my wagoneer," she said. "Have you seen him around this morning?"

"That old coot," the stableboy replied with a twinkle in his eyes. "Yes Ma'am. He's been hitched about two hours. You should put him and that off horse together. Don't know which one is the most impatient."

Lore smiled. "And my other three men who are riding out with me?"

"Oh, they got their horses not long after Mr. Benson rode out."

"Did they say where they were going?" Lore asked.

"Nope. Just paid for the keep and rode off."

Lore stepped into the saddle. She was surprised that the three men would ride off without telling her. She rode back through the gate of the fort and hitched her horse in front of the quarters.

She had just started up the steps, when she heard a buckboard coming down the street. The team was at a full gallop. The driver pulled up. He applied the lock with his foot and sawed back on the lines.

"Whooa!" he called as the team threw up their heads to catch the weight of the rolling wagon on their necks.

"As the wagon stopped two men got out of the back. They helped a third man down. With his back to her, Lore could see the bullet hole in the buckskin shirt.

"Would you open the door for us, please Ma'am?" one of the men asked. They lifted the wounded scout from the wagon and started up the steps.

Lore held the door open and followed them inside. They went down the hall to a door that had a sign above it: "INFIRMARY."

"Is the doctor in?" one of the men asked the corporal on duty.

"He's at breakfast," the corporal replied. "I'll send for him if it's an emergency. He'll fuss about being bothered if it's not."

"You send for him," the man snapped. "Got a bullet in the back that's been there two days. Needs to come out as soon as possible."

"Put him on the couch over there by the door," the corporal said. "I don't want blood on one of my good chairs."

They helped the wounded man over to the couch and sat him down. "You shoulda' stayed in town yesterday and got that bullet out," one of the men said. "The Cavalry coulda' found us."

The scout looked up. His eyes were bloodshot, his face red with fever. But when the man spoke there was fire in his voice. "When Lance Kimball signs on to guide a wagon train through, that's what he does."

Kimball hesitated and grimaced a bit as he settled himself on the couch.

"Besides, I had to get a message back to Cumby," he said.

"About that killer what's waitin fer him?" the other man asked.

"Yes," Kimball said. "I thought he'd run. I've seen Nathan Benson draw. Cumby won't stand a chance against him. And Cumby's got a job I'd hoped he could live to do."

"He ain't runnin," the second man said. "Fact is, he's probably facing Benson right about now."

Lore moved quickly across the lobby. She looked down at Lance Kimball, caught the light in his eye. He had an honest, determined face. He had risked his life to get help to the wagon train -- had ridden back with a bullet in his shoulder to lead the Cavalry to the wagons. This man would have a purpose in what he did.

"The man you call Cumby," Lore said. "The man with the wagon train. You said he had something you wanted him to live to do. Can you tell me what it was?"

Kimball looked up, studying the raven haired woman bent over him.

"Reckon I can, Ma'am," he said. "Though it don't make no whole lot of difference now. It was his daughter he's been looking for. Morning Bird, he called her. I just hoped he could find her before Benson found him."

"Morning Bird," Lore mused. "Morning Bird Cumby. That's a pretty name. Do you know how long she's been lost?"

"Close on to fifteen years, Cumby says, And he's been looking for her most of those years. I'm sure he would have found her if he hadn't got mixed up in that Benson-Parker feud."

Fifteen years. It kept ringing in Lore's ears. Fifteen years.

"Where did he lose her?"

"Down in Texas where his ranch was.

"Where in Texas?" Lore felt a throb in her throat and her voice quivered.

"Where?" she asked again. "Tell me quickly."

Lance Kimball cast a puzzled glance at this woman who had suddenly displayed so much interest in Shack Cumby.

"Down south of Waco," he said. "Near Lorena."

"Lorena," she said with a catch in her voice. "My God in Heaven. That's where Jan Raphael found me fifteen years ago this spring."

"Found you?" Kimball stared up in amazement.

"Yes," Lore said, tearing open the bag on her arm. She dug frantically down through the gold coins. It seemed her fingers would not work as fast as she wanted them to. At last she came out with a small envelope. With trembling fingers, she tore open the envelope, and came out with a tiny gold locket that dangled from a delicate chain. She clutched the locket tight in her right hand.

She shoved the bag of coins to Lance Kimball.

"Hold this for me, please," she said. "I must hurry. Where are they meeting?"

"In front of the saloon," one of the men said.

Lore flew out the door and leaped down the steps. With a singular movement she flipped the reins over her mount's neck and leaped into the saddle. She whirled the roan and raked his sides with spurs.

The surprised animal lunged out and away. She lashed at his flank with the reins, but that was not needed. A quarter horse by breeding, he hit top speed in ten seconds and thundered down the street.

Lore had heard no gunfire, yet she had the feeling that she was too late. The way her luck was running, she would be too late. She had almost gotten Jan Raphael to a doctor, but he had died the last day out. She had almost persuaded Nathan Benson to give up the chase for Shack Cumby and ride back to Texas with her. There again she had lost. Circumstances had defeated her.

Could it be that Shack Cumby was her real father? Shack Cumby, the man Nathan Benson had sworn to kill? If he was her father, the tiny locket that she clasped tight in her right hand would be the only clue to her true identity. But if she was too late she would never know. She leaned forward in the saddle.

"Hurry, boy," she spoke into the roan's ear. "Hurry just this one time for me."

As if in answer to her plea, the red roan dropped closer to the ground to stretch his stride in a new burst of speed. He came around the corner. Now he was sweeping down the street toward the saloon.

Through misty eyes Lore could see the two lines of men facing each other. Armed men facing armed men. An ominous scene. A prelude to death. She knew the story all too well. A story that had been written in blood, all across the West.

She saw the old man on the far line lift his right hand slightly and saw it streak for his gun. In the same blink of the eye there was a blur of motion above Benson's gun.

"No! Benson!" she screamed. "No! No!"

Cumby raised his empty hand, but already Benson's gun was out. Yet somehow he held the trigger finger that he had spent years training to squeeze automatically.

With the fight stopped momentarily, Lore did not slow. The sense of urgency was still too great. She barrelled between O'Quinn and Weaver, and the roan dropped his rump and did a screaming tattoo on the hard earth as he slid almost into Cumby's mount.

Shack Cumby looked down on this strange woman who had been able to stop Nathan Benson's gun hand in the middle of a draw. There was shock in his eyes, utter amazement, but no recognition.

Lore was too unnerved to talk. She hardly knew what to say, where to begin. At last she spoke softly, looking straight into the eyes of the big man.

"Your scout tells me that you've been looking for a girl you lost about fifteen years ago?"

"Yes," Cumby said slowly. "Yes, that's true. I have."

"She was lost near Lorena, the scout said."

"Just south of Lorena, on the ranch I used to own," Cumby said. "We got bushwacked by rustlers. I hid her and tried to fight them off, but I got hit. When I came around later, she was gone. I figured the rustlers took her."

"Jan Raphael found me near Lorena fifteen years ago this spring," Lore said. "He thought that I was four or five years old then."

She paused, watching the man study her.

"I don't know," Cumby said slowly. "You look something like Morning Bird's mother. But maybe that's just because I've wanted so much to find Morning Bird."

Lore was gripping the locket so tight that her fingers began to hurt.

She rode in close and thrust it out.

"I was wearing this the day Jan Raphael found me," she said.

Cumby took the locket. He opened it with a blunt thumb and held it up where he could see the tiny picture inside. He studied it momentarily, then turned to Lore.

"My God in Heaven," he said huskily "That's the locket Morning Bird was wearing the day I lost her."

146

He tried to control the tears, but when they came he smiled through them.

"My wife, Whispering Winds, died the year before I lost Morning Bird. That was the only picture I had of Whispering Winds. I placed it in a locket and put the locket around Morning Bird's neck."

"Then this picture..." Lore faltered. "This picture is.. ?"

"That picture you've carried all these years, my child, is a picture of your mother."

"But..." Lore paused. "But, I've always thought it was just a picture that came with the locket. A picture of an Indian."

"An Indian indeed, Morning Bird Cumby," Cumby said. "Your mother, the most wonderful woman God ever made, was a full blood Apache."

CHAPTER 25

The wagon rumbled south in the cool of the morning. Old Skip Bonner cracked a long whip over the backs of the team and swayed with the roll of the high seat. A trace of a smile showed on his leathery face as he looked out and away. He was on his way to Texas. He was going home.

"We're escorting the Mescaleros and their cattle down through Comanche territory," Captain Sam Scott had told Lore. "If your riders will help with the drive to where we cross into Apache land, we'll pay them for their services. We can have additional tribesmen meet us there to relieve your men so you can go on to Texas. That way we can cover your party and the drive with one escort."

So once again Skip Bonner rolled in the dust of the drag. Cattle that had swung north only a few days ago were now swinging south. South on the same trail they had travelled before.

And O'Quinn, Donnel and Weaver were once again giving forth with the melodious "Yiii! Yiii!" call of the Texan. Mingling with that was the whoop of the Mescalero.

O'Quinn, riding alongside an Apache brave, looked long at his trail companion. At last he shook his head and the red beard spread in a broad grin.

"I can hardly believe this myself," he said.

Off to the left of the drive a troop of Cavalry spread out -- riding single file by squads -- keeping pace with the string of steers. And even though the Cavalry had their own scouts out, LaRoche and Shack Cumby were out there with them.

Back of the steers and the wagon, back beyond the dust cloud that climbed up from the dry, hard earth, a woman with hair the color of a raven's wing and eyes that sparkled like dew in the early morning sun sat astride a red roan gelding. And as she rode, she smiled at the man who rode a black stud in close beside her.

Abruptly the woman pulled up, turning to her companion.

"There's something I want you to promise to do for me when we get back to Texas," she said.

"Not to give up my gun?"

"Oh no, your gun is a part of you," she smiled. "I'd never ask you to give it up."

She reached her hand across to him, and he clasped it in his own.

"When we get back to the ranch, Mr. Cumby," she paused and smiled. "That is, my Dad has promised that he will teach me to speak Apache, the language of my mother. When he does, I want you to take me to see my people."

THE AUTHOR

Edward Love Johnson, a veteran of two wars, served for a number of years as a naturalist at the world famous resort hotel, "The Greenbrier," in White Sulphur Springs, West Virginia. A taxidermist, author, banker and columnist, he served a stint as a public relations director with a circus. He is a former rodeo operator and performer. For more than fifty years, the legends, outdoor articles, animal fiction, and other writings of Johnson have appeared in many outdoor, sports, religious, and farm publications. Now retired, he continues at 96 to write, paint wildlife, garden, and make musical instruments.

www.ingramcontent.com/pod-product-compliance
Lightning Source LLC
Chambersburg PA
CBHW071258130626
46556CB00003B/1373